Making Sense of Past T
Revised Edition
Lawrence G. Taylor

Also by Lawrence G. Taylor

The Eternal Struggle: An Amorous Story
Making Sense Of Past Time
Tell Me Who My Enemy Is – a four-act closet drama
Two Girls in a Café
The Ballad of Calle and Maja -- Novella
Getting it Right, if Ever – Romance Novella
Strangers in Another Country
Four Bittersweet Romances & A Four-Act Closet Drama
Dos Chicas en un Café
Darker than Blue -- This Mortal Coil
Religion As Tormentor Of The Soul & Negative Refuge – An Essay
Binky's Reverie
A Day in The Life of Charlie Cheddar
Betty And The Black Puppy
Short Stories Novellas a Closet Drama

For my wife, son and family Anja, Ben, Sally, and Sam

Thank you, Andrea Williams, for taking the time to proof-read the text.

Copyright (c) 2018, 2022, 2023 Making Sense of Past Time – Novel by Lawrence G. Taylor.

All rights reserved.

This book or any portion thereof may not be reproduced or used in any manner whatsoever without the express written permission of the author except for the use of brief quotations in a book review.

This book is a work of fiction. Names, characters, organisations, and dialogue in the stories are the products of the author's imagination and are used fictitiously. Purely coincidental are any resemblances to persons living or dead. The views expressed in this work are solely those of the author and not necessarily reflect the views of the publisher and the publisher hereby disclaims any responsibility for them.

Quotations

That invisibility to which I refer... I am not complaining, nor am I protesting either. It is sometimes advantageous to be unseen, although it is most often rather wearing on the nerves.
 --Ralph Ellison, Invisible Man

THE WHOLE WORLD IS full of people like me, in my situation, who contain many strands, people who don't have a single, tribal identity but many identities.
 --V.S. Naipaul

WHEN A MAN BEGINS TO know himself a little he will see himself many things that are bound to horrify him. So long as a man is not horrified at himself he knows nothing about himself.
 — P. D. Ouspensky

Prologue

My 50th birthday is approaching, and I've resolved to travel back in time to make sense of the past. Following memories that specialists classify as dynamic may yet be an illusion. I am adamant that our memory is dormant. Reading also taught me that the person in our memory is easily mistaken for the person in actual life.

I periodically ponder on my history, realising inevitable mistakes and struggling to accept the awful hand fate gave me. As a result, I find myself questioning what advantage such knowledge would provide. This testimony will serve as a catharsis, leading to spiritual release.

BOOK ONE

1

LONDON, ENGLAND – 1967

Once upon a time, I migrated to a Vikland nation in pursuit of a better future after growing weary of "Inglan." I was twenty-five, but that was a very long time ago.

At just twenty, I headed to the mother country to escape my monotonous hometown and circumvent the immigration ban in Britain.

I bid farewell to a tropical landscape where I dreaded becoming caught in the hamster wheel of social mobility.

My greatest wish was to reach the shores of the United States, which would be difficult for someone like me. It was simpler to enter Britain as a British subject––thanks to history, though it was dreadful and brutal. But living in the English capital proved more difficult than I had anticipated, and I struggled to get started.

My expectations were ordinary. Get a job, have a social life, and then settle on a profession. I had graduated from secondary school, which wasn't much to brag about but enough to get me started.

Before entering the mother country, I felt assured about what to anticipate, what it meant to be a black immigrant in a white setting, and my capacity to deal with the negative and appreciate the positive.

I knew who I was and what I wanted out of life. As it turned out, I misjudged what it meant to live in a vast metropolis where racial discrimination was rampant. I thought back to my sensitivity to being judged based on race. I also became conscious of my inflated self-image, which overstated my social abilities and humorous disposition. I blamed English society, though I shouldered some of the blame.

Sunday school taught me that God created the world and that the rainbow represented the beauty of differences between nature and God's creatures. Years later, I became aware of the corruption of diversity because of human perspectives and practices.

I discovered what it was like to be black and a second-class citizen in London. While searching for work and a place to live, I became suspicious of a few practices and customs. Both cases made me suspect that preconceived notions about people of colour were at work. I could never be sure whether I had correctly perceived such situations or whether my imagination had distorted them.

Before arriving in England, I read in local newspapers about the lives of black people in Britain and America, both positive and negative. I felt prepared for the journey.

In England, flesh and blood had taken on a new dimension. Reading something seemed one thing, but experiencing it was different, which may explain some of the surprises that came my way. I had never felt such rage, shame, or self-pity.

I had to flee the motherland. My expectation of a better life outweighed my obsession with social status. I began to believe that, at best, I'd remain a stranger or become invisible in a country I adored.

My desire and attempt to be part of society had not resulted in courtesy or respect. My upbeat demeanour made no impression on the hosts and hostesses of the English metropolis: a white shirt, a striped tie and a sports jacket, and a cultivated English accent. I could not comprehend why my attempts to assimilate failed.

Discriminatory behaviour, hatred, and xenophobia disillusioned or discouraged me. I had been successful in making a few trustworthy English friends. I knew Caribbean people who were unaffected by English society. Their attention seemed drawn to something other than the negative. In retrospect, I complained about everything and everyone, including myself.

Even though I had a small group of trusted friends in Guyana, I wouldn't say I liked the capital, Georgetown, and complained about the local mentality. I complained about living in a vast and dangerous city to my well-being a few years later in the mother country.

I fantasised about being wealthy and not having to work; wealth would shield me from racial absurdity in the English environment. Because racial problems affected prominent black people, it appeared to be a childish fantasy. Still, I preferred to believe it was less so. I began to lose interest in learning a trade to rise above my station. My predicament seemed incomprehensible.

Years later, after leaving the mother country, I yearned for London's multicultural environment, despite not having had much contact with black strangers. On public transportation, I remember blacks rarely greeting each other.

I'd greet black strangers but never received a reaction. It wasn't as if I was desperate for the company or had become a lost soul. A simple hello might've brightened my day. I shouldn't blame them, for one of the disadvantages of living in a big city was not trusting strangers and wearing a mask of indifference.

Perhaps it was a city phenomenon that also affected white Londoners. I sometimes wonder how whites in Africa, the Middle East, and the Far East interacted with one another. I'd resign myself to the idea that it was a phenomenon in a dog-eat-dog environment--"the-other-is-your-hell" sort of thing.

I recall a strained relationship with many members of the English working class, even though we were both struggling to make ends meet. We were both victims. Their economic situation was comparable to mine, although our social status was difficult to compare. They benefited from social customs, values, history, and a superiority myth that favoured them.

Except for black music, the accomplishments of black athletes, and my lack of knowledge of black heroes in ancient history, I had few reasons to be proud. Their ambitions to climb the social mobility ladder might've been less vigorous than mine.

Some working-class English men claimed superiority over people of colour, which offended me. Their sense of power stemmed from myths, ignorance, and a desire to boost their self-esteem. English pride stemmed from Great Britain's historical significance on the world stage.

It was not a question of seeking dialogue or proving them wrong. Because their psychological state did not allow them: *The self-defeating futile of (sic) such engagement.* (This was Bertrand Russell's answer to Sir Oswald Mosley's invitation to a debate.)

The odd thing about the English working class was that they and I had more in common than they were willing to admit. In jest, I reflected on my pigmentation role in their lives, probably convincing them that they were no longer at the bottom of English society's social ladder.

In school, I learned more about England and less about British Guiana (Guyana). Great Britain surprised me with its magnificence, outshining BG. Some English people believed that the English language was a gift from God to people of colour.

I'd later read that the wealth generated by the North Atlantic slave trade benefited ordinary British people. But not as much as some ruling families, cities like Manchester and Liverpool, and industrialisation. Some historians believe that the Industrial Revolution might not have been possible without the success of black slavery in the New World.

In my idle thoughts, I ponder the origins of racism. Was it a result of human nature, culture, or education? Humanity has distorted the divine meaning of Earth's differences. Mortals refused to acknowledge God's good intentions.

The Jewish people have faced their fair share of prejudice and persecution. People have always needed a scapegoat.

After passing through a period of human bondage (1526-1867), the "black race" could claim or share first place.

For ...no animal could ever be so cruel as a man, so artfully, so artistically cruel – to borrow a line from Fyodor Dostoyevsky.

Some brilliant minds contended that humanity erred, while others (including me) blamed original sin.

2

LONDON, ENGLAND - 1962

I ARRIVED IN THE MOTHER country on February 14. The journey took a fortnight: first by plane to Trinidad, where I boarded the Italian passenger line Ascania and stopped off in several countries, including Jamaica, Aruba, and Madeira. Then by train from Genoa, Italy, through France and probably elsewhere. And finally, from Southampton to Victoria Station by train.

As trains came and went from Victoria Station, many people were on the move. Temperatures appeared to have levelled off now that spring had arrived. There was no snow or fog on the train to London. There were cows, horses, and sheep in green pastures.

The station forecourt and some side streets appeared wet. A flock of pigeons flew back and forth in a short flight, some navigating dangerously amid traffic. One or more of them entered the station, bobbed their heads, and stopped, searching for a morsel of food. Buses, taxis, and cyclists passed by. Crazy to ride a bike in such dangerous conditions, though no more hazardous than in my hometown.

I waited for my cousin Sam to pick me up with my big suitcase. I noticed some people of both sexes staring at me along the way. Sometimes I can't help but wonder what people who stare at me are thinking. Another newcomer springs to mind. It may have been because of how stylish I was. I--a black teenager--wore a black suit with a white tie, baggy trousers, and my landlord's oversized grey winter coat.

The rush of commuters continued, leaving no time for idle chatter, probably when residents were constantly moving, rat-race-style, with no room for a smile. Life was tough.

At length and smiling as he got out of the car, Sam appeared. "Hello, cuz!" he said, getting out of a blue Ford zephyr.

He hugged me. "Welcome to Britain!"

I said, "Thanks," and tried to look happy. As I started to carry my suitcase to the car, he grabbed it and put it in the trunk. The trunk space surprised me.

"Sorry about the wait. There's a lot of traffic even at this time of day."

"No problem," I said.

"How was the trip?"

We jumped in the car and drove away from the station, merging into heavy traffic.

"At sea, I didn't fare well," I said, frowning and yawning as though to elicit pity.

"Oh, was it?" Sam chuckled. "Mine was enjoyable, although the food was terrible."

"Yes, that too," I said. "But seasickness robbed me of many a happy day. It began with breakfast." I glanced at passers-by while trying to muster the energy for conversation.

"I was lucky, just once," Sam said. "What do you think of London, first impression?"

I paused, then said, "Well, it looks like what you see in British Newsreels." After all, it's one of the world's most well-known capitals.

In the car, I relieved myself of the heavy winter coat. Sam alluded to adding fashion to my appearance. "It would be beneficial by blending quicker in the London surroundings, not standing out as a new boy whose arrival was to beat the ban," he said and smiled.

Sam sped along roads and streets, shifting gears with his left hand and guiding the car with his right.

He said, "The sun isn't as generous as in Guyana. But don't be discouraged. There are more important things to worry about, and you will undoubtedly get used to them, as most of us who arrived earlier. London can make or break you!"

He laughed to himself, seemingly at the reality of the situation. "Achievements are there for the taking, despite negative vibes that come our way. The trick I found was to avoid becoming arrogant. Determination gets you far."

I nodded, tired and unconcerned about the important things ahead. I said I was grateful for the advice.

Was Sam preparing me for the unexpected? Should the situation prove nerve-racking, humiliating, and unbearable, I could apply for a return ticket, a secret contingency plan between my mother and me.

I was just another young man settling into London's great metropolis.

At age thirty, Sam was tall and well-built, like a bodybuilder. He married a woman from Guyana. Daphne was her name, and I'd meet her for the first time. She greeted me with a smile and a handshake, and she was pretty, tall, and slender.

She seemed confident, based on conversations with my mother and her sisters. They talked about another woman friend of Sam's, but Daphne got her man. Six years ago, Sam and Daphne moved to London. They had no children. Both worked as civil servants and took evening classes at the university. Daphne studied business administration, while Sam studied architecture.

My stay with the couple provided me with a comfortable opportunity to experience urban life for a few weeks. I'd look for a job, find a room and become an evening student in time.

I TOOK THE SUBWAY TO various tourist attractions. With the help of a tourist brochure, I visited Madame Tussauds, the British Museum, the Commonwealth Institute, Dickens House, and a few other tourist attractions. A city map was helpful.

I'd ask random people for directions, but they were sometimes willing to help. I recalled a well-dressed Englishman who was ostentatiously well-mannered but misdirected me. As a new boy, it was hard to tell if it was on purpose.

I received similar deceits delivered with politeness. I joked about it in letters to my mother and friends.

Sometimes it was easier to take the bus, but I chose the subway. I liked taking the tube train. Sam spoke of others "beat the tube" and warned me not to try it. It meant buying a ticket to the nearest station but travelling much further.

I met Sam after work on some days, and he invited me to a pub where he and some of his Caribbean friends hung out. The chat covered social topics such as parties, ladies, music, and sports such as athletics, cricket, and football. There was some discussion of racial prejudice in the workplace or elsewhere. The men talked about their experiences with humour and without anger. I stood in their midst, listening to their stories, knowing it would be my turn to tell them one day.

3

GEORGETOWN, GUYANA - the 1940s & 50s

I HAD A WEAK CONSTITUTION and picky eating habits as a kid. At the sight of some meals, I'd made a face: bonefish or biff or vegetable soup.

I liked bread and cheese a lot. I enjoyed eating cook-up rice, pepper pot, metemgee soup, a stew of salt fish and dumplings with coconut milk, cassava, plantains, yam, sweet potatoes and chicken curry and roti.

But those dishes only appeared on weekends. I had two options: eat whatever was on the dinner table or starve - a rule set by my dad. It was Christian gratitude to eat what was on your plate.

Compared to my stepbrother, Thomas, my mother remembered me as a cheeky but cheerful child. And following a scolding from our father for misbehaving, I'd regain my composure, bearing no grudges. Thomas would be sad for quite some time.

In my early adolescence, I fantasised about becoming an electrician like my mother's father or a baritone radio host. I desired to grow up, live my own life and succeed in whatever I set my mind to. Daydreaming became one of my favourite ways to pass the time.

Making new friends and socialising, playing, and sporting events were the highlights of my primary school experience.

I was a slow learner who needed help focusing, making it challenging to get good results.

There were a few other "slow boats" in my class. My pride won out and made me realise that I needed to excel in school if I wanted to succeed in the future. Some of my schoolmates were champions of excellence. I liked the thought of shining.

I recall a few driven classmates who pushed me to continue my studies with them after school. They went too far with the book learning, though. The balance of hard work and little leisure time was overwhelming for someone like me. I quit the study group because I might've settled for being average. Years later, I discovered that learning new things required effort from everyone, even geniuses.

My father didn't take kindly to my lazy attitude. He preached to me about the importance of academic learning during a spanking lesson he conducted with his belt.

He would say, "You see, master Harry, attending school is to get good grades and learn to lead a moral, obedient, productive life."

That explains why he was stern with me. He blamed the devil, my lack of ambition, and my stubbornness.

I realised then that my father would not hold me in high regard if I didn't excel in school. I might've received my dad's blessing if I had been a diligent pupil and got excellent results.

I was partly responsible. I was too much of a clown and lacked motivation. My mother was worried and prayed to the Lord. I was relieved to no longer be at the bottom of the barrel when I advanced to the average pupil level.

During a lesson, Miss Burnett, a primary school teacher, made a degrading comment about me: "My eyes were like a drunkard, and I would become nothing." My rude behaviour might have prompted her remarks.

As she spoke, she applied cane lashes to the palm of my hand. My head received a few lashes because I wasn't still.

I was happy to tell my parents about the situation. My mother found the incident horrifying and pleaded with my father to act. Unexpectedly, he appeared upset; he advised me to leave the classroom if Miss Burnett's rude behaviour continued.

It did, and I didn't think twice about following my father's advice. It might've been an act of vengeance against Miss Burnett's authoritarian, demeaning, and vicious personality. I started going to a different school.

I RECALL MY FIRST WEEK at Primary school, and before the bell struck for a lunch break, I could no longer sustain the need to hold my bladder. Instead of raising a hand to indicate my desperate need, I lost control of the situation.

The accident was shameful, but Miss Cummings handled it well by not thinking much of my incident. I don't remember being made fun of by my classmates, which was unusual for me at that age when bullying and teasing were commonplace.

The next day, Miss Cummings informed the class of the emergency procedure of going to the toilet by raising one's hand.

I once blushed a little when she made a flattering remark about my face. She was also attractive, but I refrained from complimenting her out of modesty and respect.

In hindsight, I'd have happily exchanged anything for academic excellence. I secretly wished to be as bright as some of my friends. Being a smart kid would ensure the fatherly love I needed.

To this day, I remember Miss Cummings' and Miss Burnett's comments as if the two teachers had chiselled the words onto the walls of my head. Do the words have any significance?

I started to take schoolwork seriously, even though recreational sports and other social activities were the most pleasurable things at primary school. There, I made many friends. I had occasionally encountered a rascal or someone inclined toward crime, who can make one feel fearful to the core of their being. Fortunately, I could rely on an older mentor for protection.

4

LONDON

I STARTED LOOKING FOR a job and thought I'd have no trouble finding one, even though the UK unemployment rate was 2.1%. I needed my dad to pull some strings because my confidence was declining. I kept reminding myself of my high school diploma and thought a university degree would have done wonders. But I stopped wishing and faced up to the situation.

I visited the Labour Exchange in the London Borough of Wandsworth at Sam's suggestion. He lived in Balham, which could have been within walking distance, though I doubt it.

After waiting for 30 minutes, I heard my name and headed toward an official. "Good morning, I said, smiling as I sat opposite him in a cubicle, adding: "This is my first visit."

"I'd have to register you," the English official said; his face carried no warmth, and he sounded cockney. He appeared in his thirties. I presented my passport, a union letter of recommendation, another about my profession as a Guyana court journalist, and school credentials.

During the interview, the official might have asked me the purpose of coming to the UK, how long I intend to stay and how much money I have to my name. My answers would have been honest: I have a hundred pounds and plan to work and attend evening classes.

The official asked, "What line of work are you looking for?"

"Well, something clerical or anything else for a start," I said.

"The clerk went through a file system and presented two manual job offers: at Lyon Corner House in Marble Arch and Sainsbury's (supermarket) near Gloucester Road.

"Thank you," I said, rising from my seat and exiting the building. When I travelled to the Labour Exchange, the air was colder, but now the sun provided warmth.

Twice a week, I would sign at the Labour Exchange. It will be possible to apply for social assistance or unemployment compensation in a few weeks.

My hopes were high. I hoped one of the two jobs would be for a clerk, but beggars can't be choosers.

On the way back to Sam's apartment, I stopped at a Post Office to purchase a few airmail letters and a bakery to purchase a loaf of whole wheat bread. Before going to the West End cinema, I wrote to my parents and a few friends.

I applied for the two positions the next day but am still awaiting a response. Both interviews were polite, and both places thought I was "overqualified." I smiled, thanked them for their time, and exited.

My calm and collected demeanour remained intact. But the fact that regular employment might be complex to acquire was a cause for concern. It was my wish that things would improve soon.

I kept going to the labour exchange twice a week, and once or twice a week, I got a job opening for which to apply. Sam told me to stay calm about getting a job through the Labour Exchange.

My letters to my mother bore some grievances:

- The foggy English weather
- The cold sheets without a hot water bottle
- The overt but mostly covert racial discrimination
- My dealings or reaction to any such act

I wrote that I missed my friends and family.

I took a break and might have grabbed a book from a small bookshelf to look at after writing the letters.

Sam and Daphne's apartment had a bedroom, kitchen, bathroom, and living room with floral-patterned curtains, fluorescent lighting, and plants. There were some Georgian Mahogany chairs and a brown, oblong table, and a brown five-piece sofa appeared new. I bought a collapsible cot and slept in the living room. After writing letters, I took a break. I grabbed a book from a small shelf.

Why did I decide to leave the country in which I grew up? There were no answers that made sense. The desire to return to my home country started to fade, but other feelings, like guilt and shame, made me uneasy. I began to agree with what my father said about me.

Was it a mistake for my mother to defend me out of maternal love? Negative thoughts had taken over, which I despised.

I felt upset and decided to compose myself by refraining from puerile whining. Because I needed to be responsible, I left Guyana to pursue another path. I wanted to be the master of my own life, to separate myself from my parents––the most positive and negative twin forces of my existence thus far. I'd make mistakes, but that is part of the learning process. I had to let go of the idea that life in this city would be easy and convince myself that things would improve.

I'd do what Sam suggested and look for a regular job. The concept did not appeal to me. The conviction that one must earn a living appealed to me, even if finding myself in a lower profession would not be enjoyable. I realised I needed to change my mindset.

I now needed unemployment benefits. Three months passed with no work, and reality humiliated me. I searched the London Evening Standard and the Evening News newspapers and applied for some jobs.

I went to London Transport one morning to apply for a job as a bus conductor. Several black immigrants were in the waiting room when I walked into the office. The amount encouraged me because there may have been a campaign to hire drivers and conductors. I imagined myself dressed in a neat uniform and a hat, perhaps romantically. In any case, my situation was dire. I had to fill out a form given to me by an English secretary.

After an hour, it was my turn, and an Englishman greeted me. He carried a big tummy and looked to be in his late 40s, slightly bald on top and with steel-rimmed glasses perched halfway up his thin nose. When he asked me to take a seat, his demeanour seemed friendly. He smiled as he scanned through my application and asked a few questions, including, "How long have you been in the UK? Do you have a job, a trade or something?"

"I realised the situation for trained people from your part of the world had become increasingly difficult over the years," he added. What sounded like words from a thoughtful and compassionate Englishman. I agreed on the spot. "Was the reporter's job your only work experience?" he inquired.

"Yes," I replied

Smiling and calm, the English clerk asked why I wanted to be a bus attendant. The question warranted a few seconds of reflection because I didn't wish to reveal my desperation to find work.

"I needed to be part of the British workforce," I said.

The interviewer nodded sympathetically away. He explained that many newcomers were in a similar situation.

My application was then placed in a tray of applications from his seat as he stood up, and we clasped hands. He thanked me for my interest and said I would receive an answer by mail. We parted ways.

As I walked down the street, I realised my chances of getting a job on the bus were slim.

I pondered whether the interview went well. I was sceptical. I might have appeared to be proud of my work as a journalist. My inexperience was evident; I needed a consistent routine.

I hoped luck would shine on me and promised to pray for a change of fortune. I wasn't much for praying. I did it when my mother compelled me to kneel in prayer with her.

I still considered myself a Christian, but not as religious as my mother and sister, Sandra. They both believed in the will and the power of the Almighty. I saw the world as something God created and expected His children to live according to His Word. I entered a world of eternal sin, but my inner voice was of a different order. My mother refers to my *inner voice* as Satan, the former archangel of God.

I like having someone as powerful as the devil to blame during childhood. But my father never failed to remind me of my responsibility for my sins. I eventually agreed with my father's saying that God only helps those who help themselves.

My father, like most Guyanese, described himself as a Christian, though I was sure he unwittingly followed Satan's ways daily.

Friends and I talked about who had more power in this world: God or Satan. I declared God was the Supreme, that He created the world, and that He was the source of righteousness out of fear.

However, I had a nagging suspicion that Satan possessed greater strength and a little edge and that the war between good and evil would last until the end. My mother told me that my argument stemmed from weakness.

That night, on the interview day, I dreamed of getting a cleaning job, although the country was Guyana. I felt relieved when I realised the importance of adversity and the value of starting at the bottom and working my way up.

My situation remained the same the following day. Either the devil or God is putting me to the test. I must not waver because, in my new life, it seemed as if proving my father wrong had become a compulsion as I fought for his love and respect. So, I remained firm. The goodness that exists within me will triumph.

A week had passed since the London Transport interview, and instead of waiting for an answer, I continued my search. My daily routine included reviewing job postings and selecting a few to call, write, or visit. My mandatory weekly two-day trips to the Labour Exchange continued, and I received the dole. I experienced a sense of guilt that surprised me. The Labour Exchange clerk sent me to a restaurant on the High Street in Kensington for a job as a porter. But fortune continued to dodge me.

I wore a black suit from Guyana, with baggy trousers in Guyanese parlance. They made a lot of flaps on a windy day. Sam got into teasing me about my outfit and laughed at my expense. I never took it personally because he was joking, and it was kind of him to offer me temporary accommodation.

I began to suspect that my out-of-fashion trousers might be hurting my job search performance. I wanted to make a good impression during meetings with potential employers and job interviews. I now had another thing to blame.

The job search continued the next day. I decided to swallow my pride and look for unannounced dishwasher jobs in some West End restaurants. The standard greeting, "No, no vacancy", was as if my presence revealed my intent.

The trail of refusal grew longer with each passing day. People like me fill these jobs quickly, whether they have papers or not.

My faith in success dwindled as I tried to use humour to distract myself from total despair. I laughed as I wrote a telegram-like letter to the editor of a London tabloid describing the following scene.

Diehard situation. Though of minor importance, a *young colonial subject of the British Crown entered the UK in a positive frame of mind and armed with a secondary certificate. He is in pursuit of work which eludes him for some god-damn reason. The fellow loses hold of himself and becomes disillusioned. A burst of insanity sends him into a mental disor-*

der, as fate would have it. He strips naked at the gates of Her Majesty the Queen as if it were the least he could do.

Two female police were the first law enforcement officers to arrive at the scene, chewing as if the alarm had interrupted their lunch break. They quickly shield his private part with a hat before seizing him like a wrestler and dumping him into their vehicle. The police vehicle took off at full speed, with flashing blue lights and a bellowing siren.

When the trio arrived at the psychiatric facility, the fellow without a name burst into tears and laughter. A psychiatrist rewarded him with a psychosis diagnosis.

My optimism remained, armed with a high school certificate and youthfulness. I decided to inject myself with a dose of Christian thinking, telling myself that I shouldn't be disheartened and that I'd survive the ordeal with the winds of positive change. Because of first-hand experience, they only come with a price tag.

Common sense asserted itself, advising me to take a break from the nerve-racking job search. I kept my mental health in check and avoided a mental breakdown.

Over a cup of tea and a cheese sandwich, I reflected on the pressing need for new lodging. The thought of being thrown onto the streets of London remained terrifying, but I wasn't afraid it would happen.

My presence at Sam and Daphne's house started to cause discontent. Daphne––a seemingly gentle and likeable lady––had begun to fret about my stay behind my back and made me feel invisible. I contributed £10 per month for boarding. But my three-month stay deprived them of their privacy. Daphne's feelings were understandable: I had become an uninvited guest who outlasted his stay.

The thought of becoming a burden to others struck me. As Sam described the situation, he appeared embarrassed. I apologised for the inconvenience and stated that finding accommodation would be my top priority.

5
GEORGETOWN

GUYANA HAS MANY RIVERS and a modest portion of the South American rainforest. Society is multi-ethnic. Guyana had been under Dutch or British rule at various times in its history but not under the three colonies' complete control (Demerara, Berbice and Essequibo), eventually becoming British Guiana (Guyana).

With the advent of independence on May 26, 1966, Great Britain's flag no longer wavered from government buildings' rooftops, which it had continuously done since 1831.

My parents were Samuel and Thelma Holmes, and I was the youngest of three siblings until my little sister Sandra arrived two years later. My father told his drinking buddies that my stepbrother Thomas and stepsister Faye had lost their mother, Edwina, because of bad luck. Our family was from the middle class (neither rich nor poor) in a country with a history of total oppression.

Food appeared on the table, and the family dressed nicely. My siblings and I each had our bedroom, and my parents were influential figures in their children's upbringing.

Samuel Holmes was a medium-sized man with a wiry build and a dark complexion. He had bulging brown eyes, but his face appeared handsome; he wore short hair and spoke in a baritone voice. He was a man of discipline who adored his family, as my mother always said. My father enjoyed his liquor and the company of his drinking buddies. He had a skilled pair of hands to do repairs around the house.

My mother thought I was nearly a carbon copy of him. Both Thomas and Faye had dark skin. Thomas was tall and muscular, while Faye was short and chubby. They were good-looking.

My mum's grandfather was German; his surname was Schroder. Her grandmother was an Afro-Barbadian, and her name was Beck, born in 1850. My mother had a mahogany complexion, average stature, slim and attractive looking, and wavy black hair above her shoulders. She worshipped God – "Who created the world"– and His image was white in our church and my parents' home.

During puberty, I remembered some fair-skinned friends making jokes about who was a tar baby. But hardly anyone took the label seriously, and I can't recall adults using the term.

Racial bias existed, but it wasn't as pronounced as in Brazil or the USA.

I once dreamed of being a quadroon. I used to boast that I had a great-great-grandfather from Germany (of all places). Soon I dropped the bragging after learning of all the rapes enslaved women endured at the hands of Caucasian plantation owners.

Through my history and geography classes, I became aware of the status of white people, that they ruled the world and that being white was a symbol of privilege and power.

After a decade, I discovered that not every Caucasian was privileged and powerful.

I went through most of what I found in textbooks and did not question the knowledge.

Some of my bright classmates strived to be knowledgeable and factual––having facts at their fingertips, which seemed to nourish their inflated egos.

When British Guiana became Guyana an independent nation in 1966, national pride came to the fore. I began to regard the significance of the national hero Cuffy and the 1763 Berbice Rebellion and the Demerara Rebellion in August 1823.

At school, I missed out on the importance of both historical events.

Much later, I read Christopher Columbus had sighted Guyana in 1498. But it wasn't until 1531, with an expedition led by the Spaniard Diego de Ordaz, that the Europeans entered Guyanese soil.

Those were the good old days of European imperialism, which pounced on peaceful peoples and imposed its authority over land, sea, and human merchandise.

Before that invasion and seizure of land (and what would become my country), Guyana belonged to the indigenous peoples, Amerindians (six groups, notably Warraus). Then there were enslaved people from West Africa, of whom my ancestors emerged later, in the middle of the 17th century, under Dutch or British rule.

The world became a playing field for military power countries, where a few nations jostled to conquer the new world. From the late 15th century on, Europeans joined the slave trade on the African continent.

There was the scramble for Africa, the Conquest, or its Partition. In 1870, only 10% of Africa went under European control. By 1914, it had grown to almost 90% of the continent, with Ethiopia, Somalia, and Liberia remaining independent, as I later read in the British Library.

Enslaved people were bought or captured and transported on ships owned by the West India Company. Some culprits who did the selling were Arabs (Moors). Africans were selling Africans from another tribe they had captured after a battle. But trade escalated with the involvement of European traders.

In 1580 the Dutch gained a foothold, setting up trading posts, and from 1620 the Dutch West India Company imported enslaved Africans to work on its sugar plantations. What absurdity. I thought, in tune with my rebellious frame of mind.

6
LONDON

THE SEARCH FOR A RENTED room took precedence over job hunting. In a week of intense searching, I encountered a string of regret and deception. Eventually, a seemingly 55-year-old Polish landlady in Stockwell offered me a room for £3 per week. The location was four Tube stops away from Sam's on the Northern Line.

I recall the landlady's son, Josef, around my age, who was a big fan of the pop group The Shadows. He and I talked about English pop music, especially Cliff Richard, Alma Cogan, and Dusty Springfield. He introduced me to two pirate radio stations, Radio Caroline and Radio Luxembourg.

I walked from Sam's flat to my new place in about an hour, if not longer. The weight of my packed luggage on foot caused blisters on my palms. When I arrived at the building, I regretted not taking a taxi, even though the reason was the cost of a taxi. Then there was a physical energy drain with two flights upstairs because there was no lift. It was another strain on my palms.

I remember throwing myself onto an unmade bed, my eyes rolling, the crooked cracks in the high ceiling, and an awful pattern on the grey wallpaper. The agony of finding new lodging was over. My mind wandered as I dozed off.

I concluded that most West Indian homes were like this. You had to become accustomed to damp walls and dreadful wallpaper. I remember a window rattling with a strong wind, and it was hard to open, as if it were just for show. The floor squeaked, and a door let in a draught. I tried not to think about these flaws, one of the costs of leaving my tropical home.

I made my bed and decided I should stop fretting. Then I was back at it. The creaking or squeaking sound from the bed bothered me.

My bed in Guyana was better, and I wondered who was sleeping in it now. In my room, my mother wrote, she sewed clothes for customers. It could also become her haven from my father's thunderous snoring.

I unpacked my clothes and realised I needed more hangers for shirts. Later, I visited a grocery store for bread, butter, eggs, cheese, barley water (lemonade concentrate), Ovaltine and coffee. I ordered milk from the dairy farm, and a milkman delivered it daily to the building's front door.

I recall returning home from some coffee bar in the early morning hours with friends and stealing milk from a couple of South Kensington residents.

Sam thought my rent was reasonable. Despite my complaints about my room, I got used to my first bedsitter. I was fortunate to live in a relatively densely populated immigrant environment. I felt the need to be among people of colour. I considered Brixton but decided against it after Sam informed me about the area's crime and history of racial conflict. The market was well-known and sold many Caribbean products.

I considered myself green when dealing with racial prejudice and discrimination. It took me some time to adjust to the absurdity. Choosing a seemingly integrated or predominantly West Indian environment may not have made a significant difference.

Better to face your problems rather than avoid them, Mr Brown might have said. He was one of the high school's competent teachers. Problems are indeed part of human existence.

My preference for Stockwell became problematic; there were probably personal or social reasons, not racial issues. Racial issues were likely to crop up everywhere. I turned away from the thought.

7
GEORGETOWN

PAUL, MY ENGLISH PRESCHOOL playmate, bought me shaved ice with red syrup from a street vendor. Paul sucked the shaved ice before giving it to me. I accepted the treat, and I don't remember at the time what I thought of his unsavoury behaviour. I might've been grateful.

Paul's mother sent me his used toys when I didn't get any from Santa. My mom may have inspired this kindness. Mrs Holmes and Paul's mother were Methodists.

Because of my dad, Santa wasn't there, and I didn't remember the reason for the punishment.

As a child, I recall adults (of both genders) engaging in street brawls over seemingly trivial matters. Quarrels would escalate into fights, as if one's reputation was at stake, settling scores in the style of Hollywood westerns and black and white gangster films.

After school, away from teachers, I had a few fistfights. As expected, the loser would request the fight to end.

SOME PEOPLE'S LIVES were significantly improved with academic achievement, or other advantages brought about by birth and wealth, reinforcing the status quo. I continued to perform at a mediocre academic level. I wasn't a bright kid, falling behind many of my classmates.

I judged myself against the brightest and best. Some of my classmates did the same thing, because they wanted to be the best and brightest.

My father worked as a foreman in the compositing department of a national newspaper. He was strict and vain. When I was younger, I thought he was the most authoritarian father in the neighbourhood.

Corporal punishment influenced my life and did more harm than good. My stubbornness continued into adulthood, manifesting as a self-destructive pattern like tantrum throwing.

My father was typical of most fathers in Guyana. He was not an evil person, and he did what he believed was right.

Many single mothers used to slap the face, head, or belt to discipline their children. Teachers, male and female, were no exception. I'm unsure if the practice began during colonial rule or persisted throughout the centuries.

I recall feeling tense in my father's presence, which concerned my mother, as were my siblings. I need to find out how severe their punishments were.

My mother frequently stated that her children adored and respected their father. He provided his family with food, shelter, and a sense of belonging. My mother's opinion of my father should not be dismissed or belittled. Unlike many fathers, my father appeared to be a caring husband.

Thelma Holmes was polite and likeable; she had a soft and gentle soul and was a devout Methodist. She was not an argumentative person and avoided most disagreements. She maintained her composure and showed no signs of being easily provoked. Those were the thoughts of my mother's three sisters – the Travers: Angelic, Eunice, and Macy. Thelma was the eldest.

My three maternal aunts told me it was at work, at a daily newspaper, where my parents met. My dad was the printing department foreman, and my mom worked in the bookbindery. Mr Holmes was charismatic and left an impression. Thelma Travers became his second wife.

My mum had gone to high school and seemed smarter than my dad––I remember thinking about it at age sixteen. My father appeared knowledgeable about practical matters.

As was the norm, he was the head of the household, and my mother seemed to submit to him. It was my mother's way. She appeared to be the ideal partner for my father, who seemed sure of himself.

"I must ease up with dress-making and voluntary work at the church," my mother said. She remarked to a neighbour (a Portuguese Guyanese housewife) while hanging clothes on the lines in her backyard. Naturally, there was a full-time household to manage for her, along with four siblings and customers' sewing orders. My mom was a remarkable person. A grin formed on my face. Because she was so eager to assist others, I didn't believe her.

Paul's mother, Mrs Therese Summers, and another neighbour, Ruby, helped run a Bible study group.

As she tucked me in at night, my mother would say, "I love my family dearly: Master Harry, my wayward son and Sandra, and Thomas and Faye and your dad. To God be the glory!"

I meant the world to her. Some say I learned from her that I was born with a roar of rage, a child's first trauma. I realised how protective she was of me as I approached puberty.

My mother said Sandra had our mother's personality, and I had my father's. Sandra didn't see herself that way and didn't like hearing it, and I didn't think I resembled my dad.

Sandra had a light complexion like her mother's and her mother's soft, wavy black hair, which rested just below her shoulders. Her eyes were brown, and she had a straight nose and thick lips.

She was brilliant (as my father had reminded me). When she was four, she went to a private preschool. I envied her enthusiasm for learning. At age seven, I enrolled at Kingston Methodist Primary School.

Sandra's academic performance has steadily improved over time. My mind wandered into daydreams, comic book superheroes, Mandrake, Phantom, or heroes rising from the celluloid screen like the Lone Ranger, Batman, and Flash Gordon.

My mother judged us from the goodness of our hearts. I remember her describing herself as her father's (Grandpa Adam's) favourite daughter. My mother told me that she understood the privilege she received compared to her sisters. She never appreciated it and did her best to offer her sisters moral support while they grew up.

I didn't measure up to Sandra and was embarrassed to be compared to her. I remember my father describing me as lazy.

IN ENGLAND IN THE 1960S, I scored 125 on the IQ test. As expected, Sandra's rating is higher. The results showed I had "extraordinary verbal skills," "could understand complex issues easily," and "a creative problem-solving approach."

I learned that a high emotional IQ is a key to success and happiness. I could have been more brilliant, but my above-average grades helped me stop underestimating myself. I wanted to see how low my score was and if I was too hard on myself.

The intelligence test, however, didn't benefit me. It's not surprising that I still consider myself ordinary, given that I continually compare myself to Sandra and my former bright schoolmates.

My father considered me a slacker.

8

LONDON

THE REJECTION LETTER from London Transport only added to my misery. I looked locally and further afield. My despair, however, subsided. Something caused me to slow down while remaining courageous.

My brother urged me not to give up hope. Thomas was still in Guyana but had no plans to study in the mother country.

My mother's letters were a source of spiritual comfort for me.

My father wasn't much of a letter writer, so his advice-laden greeting reached me via my mother and Sandra.

I coveted those who appeared to be employees on buses, trains, and sidewalks because I yearned to be a part of the workforce.

I started filing rejection letters in case the Labour Exchange doubted my efforts. My shame had subsided somewhat. The power of thoughts over emotions surprised me. I noticed a newspaper advertisement for a lower-ranking post on the West Indian Federation Interim Commission, of which British Guiana (Guyana) was a member.

I didn't waste time. I rang up immediately and got time for the interview. It was the next day, and the job was temporary. I didn't mind that because I wanted to escape the rotten luck.

Every morning, I joined the crowd of commuters heading for the subway. I purchased The Telegraph, an independent conservative newspaper I chose because of its layout and news coverage. At the time, I had only a rudimentary understanding of politics.

(I recall the first parliamentary elections in British Guiana (Guyana) in 1953. I must have been twelve. And for some reason, I rooted for Mr D'Aguiar, a Portuguese owner of a soft drink & rum company, to do well. But his party had not done so. Tears welled up and fell from my eyes. And in the years that followed, I searched vainly for an explanation for my tears of sadness. One plausible explanation was that my parents voted for him. I settled for that.)

I'd take the Northern Line to Edgware or High Barnet on my way to work. I switched to the Bakerloo Line at Elephant & Castle, finally opted for the Central Line, and got off at New Bond Street station. I was proud to be part of the British workforce, hustling and bustling in the daily traffic jam.

Initially, I was an office messenger. I occasionally did clerical work to boost my fragile self-esteem. However, such tasks were secondary.

After three months, I got the sack––just like that––for not showing up for work on Monday. I'd gone to see a Guyanese friend in Cambridge over the weekend and missed the last train back to London on Sunday. I overslept the next day and arrived late for work.

I'd be lying if I'd called in sick. It would, however, have made no difference. I got fired and learned from a trusted colleague that a senior staff member had complained about my tardiness and taken advantage of the opportunity to get rid of me.

A fellow Guyanese, a woman of Chinese, ancestry ordered the sacking. I was irritated and felt like a victim. Despite the low pay, I was proud to be doing tasks that went beyond my original position as a messenger. The important thing was that I could find work in the United Kingdom, which boosted my confidence and well-being. My job confirmed that I was a worthy member of British society. All of this, however, proved inconsolable.

The day I lost my job, self-degradation kicked in. I bought two bottles of red wine from the Off-License and went straight to my lodgings. Within an hour, I consumed a bottle of wine and made a racket: laughing at my cynical jokes about others and singing like Nate King Cole. The homeowner wasn't home, but some tenants became upset.

The following day, a loud knock on my door woke me up. Usually, I wear pyjamas, but now I only wear briefs. I zigzagged sleepily towards my door, a blanket wrapped around my lower body. After almost tripping on the bedspread edge, I mumbled before opening the door. The landlady's son was standing there.

"Oh, so you're still home!" Josef said before I could ask what was wrong. I'd been knocking for a while and was getting nervous." He appeared concerned when he handed me a folded piece of white paper.

"What exactly is this?" My brow furrowed as I inquired.

"It's from my mother. I'm in a hurry!" The next thing I knew, he descended the stairs in long strides.

"Oh, okay," I mumbled as I closed the door and unfolded the white paper. It said, *Last night, you offended other guests with your noisy behaviour. I'm now serving you a week's notice to vacate the room.* I felt the urge to get dressed and present an honest apology to the Polish landlady. It looked, however, like it was too late.

I got myself into a bind. I'd lost my job and would soon be homeless. Misfortune never comes alone, says the Russian proverb.

Was I becoming like my dad? Not drinking, I mean, but his angry manner. I detected a slight change in myself: impatient and arrogant. That was how I might have appeared to my mum, friends, and classmates, who occasionally agreed to fight after school. I wasn't always disappointed whenever I lost, as though the defeat served as penance.

During an intensive search for new lodging, I received recommendations from West Indian friends in a pub in Leicester Square. I soon found a single room on Cromwell Road, near Earl's Court Road. The building housed a few Guyanese, and the neighbourhood had a cosmopolitan atmosphere with black and white foreigners. It was pleasant to meet West Indians, Africans, Australians, and Americans, primarily globetrotters.

Being unemployed again hadn't affected me as much as it did in the first few months. Some officials at the Labour Exchange appeared less critical and more mindful of my plight. I considered myself fortunate to have dealt with sympathetic officials, mostly women whom I affectionately referred to as maternal types. It struck me as a divine blessing. The sacking was a lesson to be learned through my mother's eyes. She stated that God would guide you through adversity if you do not turn your back on him. So, I hoped and believed that something better would come. I had some reservations about following in her footsteps in life. How do you stay true to yourself while meeting your parent's expectations? In retrospect, it was much concern to me.

9
GEORGETOWN

SANDRA'S SUCCESS CONTINUED to be my father's yardstick for assessing my academic ability. *You cannot match a well-mannered, bright child by not working twice as hard.* The words were my father's wisdom while handing out lashes for misbehaviour or poor test results. Or for my stubbornness, which did not serve me well. The punishment impacted the women in the household who pleaded for a less severe sentence but to no avail.

In times like these, I wished my father would leave this world on a Beelzebub-powered express train because I lacked the courage to enter the annals of parricide. The gods, however, refused my request by turning a blind eye. In solitude, and on and off, I shed tears for being a coward. My Christian faith might have rescued me from the jaws of disgrace.

Sandra finished secondary school at the age of eighteen. She completed eight O-level subjects in one sitting, followed by three A-levels. She then attended a private short-hand and typing school for one term before beginning her career as a civil servant at the Ministry of Education. Sandra became engaged to Mark Evans a few years later. Mark had a dark complexion, a similar background, and worked in the justice department. Sandra's family was proud of her academic success, for which she was "responsible," as my father put it.

My father disciplined me in my early teens. My mother informed me that Thomas had also received numerous beatings for misbehaviour and poor academic performance. Thomas stated that "spanking had served me well." He once boasted about the benefits of flogging for our father's drinking buddies. I may have muttered a curse under my breath.

"Harry," Thomas once said to me, having the audacity. "Such discipline produces favourable outcomes. You will reap the rewards, as I have."

Looking up at him, I remarked, "Therefore, I'm likely to stray without spankings and lectures. Is that it?"

"There you have it, young man!" He laughed. "You're not as sluggish as our father makes you out to me."

"Thanks a lot, Thomas. You should enlighten our dad."

"I believe our father already knows. He is concerned and cares for you. But you don't appear appreciable. It's just that our father has a problem with disobedience, especially from children. Our father blames the company you keep! After all, he is our father. No adult likes a rude child. Our father wishes us all well!"

It was now time for me to leave for school. I had a good excuse for not appearing impolite to my stepbrother. Was I grateful for such sibling insight? I needed clarification. He got on well with our dad. Thomas was twenty-two and worked at the Royal Bank of Canada. He planned to enrol at Howard University to study chemical engineering. I had good reasons to be grateful to our dad. I was a fourteen-year-old ungrateful brat. I didn't care.

Possibly I was a rebel, a troubled youth (like James Dean in the film Rebel Without a Cause), probably with a grudge to bear. An axe to grind.

I realise now my problem was a sense of not belonging. The punishment I received appeared to strengthen my stubbornness. Occasionally, after receiving a spanking, I wished I could die there and then.

Later in life, I pondered the origins and persistence of my pig-headedness in situations where my response was infantile and absurd. I couldn't determine whether the stupidity was part of my genetic make-up or nurtured.

During a motherly moment of consolation, I remembered my mum telling me that my stepsister Faye had once been 'daddy's favourite.'

Perplexed, I approached Faye from the kitchen for confirmation. She was reading The Daily Chronicle Newspaper in the living room. With a smile, I apologised for the interruption.

"Yea," she said, looking up and adding, "What prompted the question?"

"Oh, nothing. Just a thought," I said, slightly embarrassed.

"Well, yes. Our dad did," Faye reiterated. "But fathers can be like that," she said and did not shift her gaze away from the paper. She was sitting in the living room and now looked up at me. "I remembered my girlfriends and me at school praising our fathers and wishing to marry someone like them because we thought they were special. I idealised them," she laughed.

I turned to her, and she gave me a glance of curiosity before giggling.

"What happened when it finally stopped?" I said as I rubbed my temples.

Faye, sitting on a couch with the newspaper, speculated that the time could have been around the birth of their younger sister Sandra. Sandra was such a cute little kid, I remember. Even though you're too young to remember, we all loved our little sister."

Finally, mustering up the nerve to ask, "Was I ever my father's favourite?"

"Of course you were, Harry! What motivates such a question? When you were born, your father was very pleased. Thomas and I may have been envious of you," insinuating a grin.

I was interested in Faye's perspective on a father's dwindling feelings for her.

"Not that it hurt my feelings or anything, Harry. I had a social life and was flattered by the advances of several young men. For a short time, it's normal for a father and a daughter to be smitten with one another." The thought of that time in her life brought on a smile. "I was no longer a child."

Faye seemed genuinely interested in my questioning.

I said, "I only wanted to know," adding that I'm far from being my father's favourite.

"Don't take it to heart, Harry. It's only a passing phase, an indulgence. In a way, we all are Daddy's favourite! He's proud of us all. We're no longer infants, Harry."

Faye was right, in retrospect. My need for fatherly love, the belief it was lacking in my life, would follow me like a shadow. At work, I got into arguments with older men but not with older women. I once talked about it with a priest, but I can't remember what he said.

Faye and I got along well. Like my mum, she would listen to my troubles with our dad and school problems. She aspired to be a nurse and worked at the Ministry of Health. Faye wasn't much for office work, though. "I want to practice health care," she said.

Faye and her stepmother were not close, but she rarely displayed disrespect. I couldn't discern the nature of my mother's relationship with Faye. It may have been due to their unique chemistry or because she had lost her mother at a young age.

Faye and my mother were not that dissimilar. Did Faye feel unloved by our mother? Now, the thought occurred to me. I don't remember asking her, nor would I dare to do so. Faye was a loving sister to her siblings and adored our father. They appeared to have confided in the other.

On the veranda, the father and daughter engaged in conversation. Faye did most of the listening; in this regard, she was comparable to my mother. Perhaps better than our mother, whose mind seemed to wander while her spouse rambled about work-related issues and personal opinions.

My mum once told me that Grandpa Adam's great-great-grandparents were the 2nd generation to have "escaped" slavery. There was some attempt to do a family tree, but the task seemed intractable, with insufficient information and know-how. I was curious to learn of my father's great-grandparents, but my mum had heard little or nothing of substance to offer me. Perhaps the reason was due to my dad's mortification. I'm not sure.

My father was not particularly interested in discussing slavery. "Some things are better left unsaid," he once remarked during my attempt to get him to talk about it. I was bemused by his demeanour. Slavery affected around twelve million Africans for 300 or more years. Then, years later, I became ashamed and sad, as my father might have been, of that colossal human tragedy.

10

LONDON

I MADE NEW FRIENDS, West Indians, at a dance at the Commonwealth Institute. One of them was a Jamaican engineering student, Percival. He told me about the West Indian Student Centre, which was within walking distance from my new accommodation. The Student Centre was a beautiful Victorian building, serving lunch and dinner at an affordable price for students, associate members, or guests. The low-cost meal and social mingling made me a frequent visitor, and the Student Centre offered other facilities. I use a table tennis room and a shower twice weekly in the basement. On the ground floor was ample space for lectures and dances, a TV room, and an adjoining study on the first floor. I immediately applied for associate membership since I wasn't a student.

At dances at the Student Centre, I became acquainted with a few women. One was a Spanish woman in her forties or older, for there were bags under her eyes. I flirted with her while dancing and wondered whether we could meet sometime. But I got nowhere because she considered me much too young. A similar result came from a Guyanese nurse student after I declared that I had no interest in studying.

A third dance partner, who came from one of the smaller Caribbean islands, wanted to know what I was doing for a living. I said that I work as a restaurant dishwasher with a wink, crossed my fingers and added that I hoped to get promoted soon.

I only got a single dance before she turned her back on me. I remember being satisfied because I wanted to try my luck with women from Europe. I had developed an interest in Continental women, mainly from Italy.

In Guyana, the Italian actress Sophia Lorene was one of my favourite Hollywood actresses; tall and thick, Eva Gardner and Deborah Kerr were appealing. Good-looking or classy English girls, I considered standoffish. I wanted elegant chicks. It was as if feminine beauty (like wealth or owning a Ferrari car) would enhance my social status.

Of course, there were attractive-looking English working-class girls, but I found it embarrassing to flirt with them, which had to do with my snobbish attitude. I couldn't appreciate how they dressed, talked, and laughed at that time. There was to be no difference between them and the lower-class girls in my hometown. I recall how I behaved like a snob, pure and simple. My attitude reminded me of a friend in my hometown who talked about my vanity.

I attended a few discos and clubs in the West End. The Flamingo, the Marquee Club, and others. Discotheques, dance halls, coffee bars, pubs, and parks became familiar places to meet girlfriends.

I met Sean, a Jamaican who visited the Student Centre. He had crossed eyes, a full beard and probably was in his forties. Sean was charismatic and always had a story to tell, which entertained me and others. He seemed lucky to meet women from Australia and America and described himself as Casanova or Valentino. Sean was a painter; his studio was in Earl's Court. Before intimacy, he ensured the woman took a shower and proceeded uninhibitedly. He seemed like a man of the world because my limited experience of sexual affairs did not coincide with his. But I enjoyed listening.

11
GEORGETOWN

UNDOUBTEDLY, I FELT like a loser among my siblings, the unhappy family member. My dad compared me to my bright friends regarding academic achievements, which did a disservice to my self-confidence and self-esteem. The feeling of being an underdog haunted me for decades.

I disliked people comparing me, even though I continued to match myself with others. Thomas and Faye had taken Cambridge exams in secondary school. I eagerly awaited elementary school graduation, but poor grades held me back.

My father called me a "hopeless, lazy, absent-minded child." In retrospect, my problem was inattention and inability to sit still. Why did poor grades bother him?

My dad was no different from most dads in Guyana, many of whom judged their children strictly on academic achievement. I had let him down.

Years later, I saw his disappointment as linked to his pride because his children seemed to be an extension of him. Being average wasn't good enough. My father believed that academic excellence measured self-fulfilment. He had told my mother I'd never fill Sandra's shoes. The constant comparison was far too much, even for my mother. But she was unable to put a stop to it.

"What else is there to do?" That came from my dad, a father who did everything he could. Hope seemed to desert him.

What would become of me? I hadn't a clue. My mother had no answer, only hope from above. I might have thought to myself. The *Almighty could make a difference by freeing me from the devil's influence.*

My dad abruptly ceased speaking to me. I was relieved when the punishment and preaching stopped. I had the feeling I had won the battle. But the feeling of being a stranger in Mr Samuel Holmes' house lingered. It was to be my responsibility to change the situation.

My mother hoped I would outgrow my wayward ways. "Some children are like that, with the problem of a wandering mind and restless soul," she told my father. "Your son, Harry, is likeable and friendly with others; some mothers spoke highly of his manners. He enjoys sports such as athletics and cricket, and he loves birds and nature."

Like any devout Christian, my mother prayed at home and church for a change in my father's heart so that he would have compassion for me. She had prayed for me as well.'

My mother tutored me in mathematics, and her assistance was invaluable. She showed patience. She did not, however, have time to go to the market or the grocery store since she had a lot on her plate. My morning chores were to carry the groceries before going to school. She made lunches and dinners (known as "breakfast" in most households).

There was family washing, except for specific trousers and suits for my father's and Thomas' laundry. Sandra and I'd drop them off at a Chinese laundry on our way to school and pick them up on Saturdays. My mother used to sew dresses and skirts for girls and women as an extra source of income for the family. She also helped the church by teaching Sunday school and attending Mass on Sundays, in addition to caring for her four children.

My mum's prayers appeared beneficial. I passed my elementary school final exam, which showed progress. It reinforced my mother's desire for me to attend secondary school as well. She offered to pay half the term fee, and her father (Grandpa Adam) agreed to pay the remainder. My father, on the other hand, would have none of it.

My dad then decided, almost against his will, to support the idea of sending me to high school. However, my father's belief that it would be "a waste of money and the teacher's time" persisted. He said it was against his "better judgment" and that I would be better off finding a menial job.

"Money doesn't grow on trees," he reminded his family.

Thomas agreed with my father, while Faye and Sandra decided with my mother.

My mother might have been concerned about my frail physique, soft hands (like hers), weak, supple arms, and skinny torso, all of which did not prepare me for heavy physical work.

"An academic certificate would be beneficial to Harry. It would increase my chances of getting an office job," she insisted. Her argument for my survival as an adult was to settle for moderate mental duties.

Surprisingly, I wanted to attend high school to be with my friends. I recall being unconcerned about the future and more interested in prestige and glamour than in another certificate with all the hard brain work attached.

Some of my ambitious friends, Benny, Luke, and Winston, were expected to attend high school.

On the other hand, David, John, Eddie, and Robby would choose low-status jobs. The latter group appeared to be proud of their lack of ambition. They branded themselves as having fewer brains than others. Their honesty impressed me. I considered being like them, not concerned with certification and all that. That was my childish desire to imitate characters in films played by James Dean and Marlon Brando—the life of an outsider. I secretly accused my parents of not knowing "proper folks."

Some classmates boasted about their parents being able to pull strings in high places. Some may have been honest, while others may have strayed from the truth.

Low-status manual labour never seemed attractive to me. However, I had no problem socialising with friends who did such work. I may have developed snobbish views when I was fifteen or sixteen, though I was unaware of it. I knew I wanted to rise a step or two higher on the social status ladder than my father.

There was a half-baked ambition to be a singer. I've been a chorister since the age of thirteen. At sixteen, I entered a singing contest on the "Ovaltine Teenage Show" on Radio Demerara, the only radio station at the time. My fantasy did not fare well due to stage fright. Johnny Mathis, an American singer, was my favourite. I competed with a few others in my neighbourhood to be known as the local JM. I eventually abandoned the idea, resigning to the fact that I lacked the necessary skills to fill the shoes of my favourite singer.

I showed much promise in athletics, especially in the 100- and 200-meter sprints. I performed admirably. However, there was no development support available. At school, athletics were about "natural talent," with no coaching or training. Of course, I didn't take matters into my own hands by joining a sports club, possibly due to my aversion to discipline and strenuous work.

It would've undoubtedly diverted time from socialising with friends. Furthermore, I needed more stamina to put forth the effort required to complete anything worthwhile.

12
LONDON

MY UNEMPLOYMENT IRRITATED me, but I remained patient and accepted the situation for what it was. I kept my positive attitude.

I made new friends in Earl's Court and was astonished by their lifestyle. Some had a steady job in the past and managed to find work when their unemployment benefits expired, while others were on the dole for a more extended period but seemed unfazed by reality. How did they accomplish this?

I never asked them because I wasn't interested in fiddling with the system or following a similar pattern in life. In Earl's Court, there were West Indian students with whom I struck up a friendship. Out of curiosity, I continued to associate with petty criminals.

I had known a few good-for-nothings in Guyana, mostly from my neighbourhood. I would spend time on street corners in their company to kill time or to listen to their conversations. Conversations mostly revolved around movies, sports, and dating experiences. One or two arguments would lead to a fistfight somewhere to settle the matter.

A handful had procreated left, right, and Centre. Drinking and womanising were regular pastimes for some or most of them. One or more held a steady job or part-time, while others worked whenever the opportunity arose. I couldn't help but wonder what their lives were like when they attended school.

The criminals in Earl's Court were petty and hardened, desiring a comfortable life without having to work a single day. Some had only completed primary schooling, while some had received an excellent secondary education--better than mine. The latter had previously studied for a profession, such as law or business administration. I learned that from their usual boasting about one thing or another. Their ambitions had veered off course due to racehorse gambling, womanising, or becoming criminals. Some had served time in prison for false cheques, home burglary, or pimping.

The petty criminals were skilled at shoplifting. They made it appear effortless, doing mostly groceries and off-licence wine. I occasionally visited their homes, socialised, and consumed stolen food and wine.

My shoplifting started when they began jokingly calling me a "sponger" but mostly a "wimp". It stemmed from my aversion to shoplifting.

However, unhappy with their negative impression of me, I dared to demonstrate that I wasn't. My male pride was on the line. Compared to the other advanced stuff they were doing, shoplifting, though illegal, seemed like a joke.

I quickly mastered the art of shoplifting. I only stole food and wine from the off-licence, which I keep primarily hidden in the inner pockets of my Mackintosh coat.

The free items I received gave me joy and the opportunity to save money on food, and my shoplifting became a habit. A few months later, a plainclothes security guard would have apprehended me if a friend hadn't sent me a warning signal.

After nearly being caught, I decided to part with the *bad apples*. I cursed myself for having chosen such a group of friends. My foolish indulgence had come to an end. It was a rude awakening that scared the hell out of me. I thought about my parents: the shame and disgrace. It would have been entirely my fault: the situation had nothing to do with my upbringing.

My reaction might have been excessive in retrospect. As a first-time offender, I'd almost certainly get a warning. Nevertheless, I did not want my name to appear in police files. I remained grateful to Jim, a *bad apple* from a respected and well-known Guyanese family. I was always afraid of ending up in jail.

13

GEORGETOWN

I WAS DOING BETTER in high school. My grades were above average, and the prospect of discrediting my father motivated me. Still, I realised that my dislike for my father could endanger me.

My dad insisted he was always right about things.

I remember talking about my father with my close friends. Luke's father appeared to be an ideal father who was loved and did not seem to exaggerate his paternal duties. Luke's dad was unlike Benny's, Winston's, or mine. The respectful fathers of David, John, Eddie, and Robby were victims of excessive alcohol consumption and often seemed to overstep their authority.

I'd admit that my personality was like my father's. My mum perceived kindness and generosity in me. Still, she was concerned about my manner, characterised by a quick temper and stubbornness. I began to pray for a positive change, but I wasn't good at praying. I mostly begged to alleviate my fear of God's wrath and to remove my guilt through confession.

What exactly were my true feelings for my dad? I wasn't sure at times. In the heat of an argument, I held him in contempt; it was sometimes difficult for me to understand my emotions. I wouldn't be able to admit my love for him. I know when I watch a film about a father and son reconciling their tumultuous relationship. As I found refuge in the notion that a mother's relationship is more vital, I felt a twinge of sadness and tears.

Later in life, I realised the significance of the father-son bond.

Being able to attend high school boosted my self-image and well-being, and I suspected my father may have noticed the positive change.

But he'd be the last to admit it. "The act of putting a cat in the oven does not make it a loaf of bread" ––a prime example of Samuel Holmes' wit.

I managed to get four O-levels, but maths wasn't one of them. I was disappointed. My friends in the study group, Benny, Luke, and Winston, were able to rejoice in their accomplishment of six passes. Their goal was to study at Howard University.

Even though they were sad about my math grades, they reminded me that four passes were better than none.

Sandra was supportive but dismissive of my grumbling. She showered me with words of sympathy and wisdom. I sensed opprobrium flowing through my veins but managed to harness a wounded pride. I hugged my little sister and thanked her.

In hindsight, I had expected better results for the time and effort that went into the study. It was as if I had converted into a perfectionist overnight, eschewed social events in preparation for the exams, and acted responsibly enough to pat myself on the back.

Years later, I discovered that hard work didn't always guarantee you the fruits of success.

My mum wasn't dissatisfied with my results, and my dad appeared surprised. Thomas and Faye congratulated me.

My mother prayed for me on the Sunday before the exam and ensured I wore a white shirt, a cream-chestnut-striped tie, khaki pants, black socks, and yachting shoes every school day. She made sure my bag carried books, pencils, a pen, an ink bottle, eraser, and would kiss me good luck and remind me to continue to face up to my burdensome tasks.

My mother said she prayed extra on the exam day after I rushed through the door and onto my second-hand Raleigh bicycle. I saw her standing there as I looked back to wave goodbye. My mother told me later that she kept standing by the door until I was out of sight. She had done everything she could for me; it's no surprise that I adore her.

Her husband remarked that his wife had over-mothered me. On the other hand, Thelma Holmes seemed sure that she was acting out of love and God's will.

His wife may have loved God more than him.

Later in puberty, I observed a difference in the relationship between my parents in the emotional sense. My father grew tired of my mother, or she lost faith in him. My parents still talked, though not as they used to, chatting, cuddling, hugging, laughing, and listening to music on the gramophone or a talk show on the radio.

My mother continued her domestic and family duties and supported her children. Knowing my mum, the servant of God she was, she must have prayed for her passion for my dad to return, blaming herself and fearing the wrath of God. It was only my belief she might have taken refuge in the idea that the Lord had willed it that way, that Samuel Holmes had failed her and me. I believed Thelma Holmes trusted the Lord and hoped he would understand her and her children and not let them down.

14

LONDON

I INSTANTLY SOUGHT lodging with two decent buddies – a fellow Guyanese and a Saint Lucian in their late thirties. Their flat was in a less fashionable part of Chelsea known as the "World's End." I had befriended them at the Lutheran Church during a social evening gathering.

My parents had always warned me about mixing with the wrong company. Although I wasn't blind to the risks, I lacked a proper understanding of my attraction to an undesirable company in my youth. Was it an unconscious desire to cast off the shackles of Christian morality? I wasn't sure.

Years later, I thought back on my blunder. Had it been out of curiosity for the *bad apples'* down-to-earth manner, choosing, as it were, to swim against the tide? Was it that I had over-romanticised their antisocial behaviour? Was it some form of rebellion against white society? Whatever the reason, it was contrary to my idealistic and romantic view of life.

My theft continued, much to my dismay, and I had no idea how to stop it. While shopping, I felt tempted to pinch one or two items. I usually managed to resist the urge. But when my self-control failed me, I carried out the act, counting myself lucky. Like any compulsion, it stuck with me. I consulted books, searching for a quick cure. Was it kleptomania? Is it possible to become a kleptomaniac by habit or be born like that? Was it an addiction that could be unlearned? My willpower wasn't serving me well. My prayers went unanswered. I dared not ask my two respectable roommates for advice for fear of being thrown out of the apartment.

I had sought help from a priest of the Lutheran Church. I had approached him as he was about to leave the Church premises on his bike. He was a kind and gentle person, always willing to help. The priest gave me a few minutes of his time, bringing me to my senses in a simple but skilful manner. He presented the pros and cons of my problematic situation and spared me the talk of sin, the devil, and the rest. He pointed out that the advantages were short-lived, while the disadvantages were likely to be permanent.

"We all have flaws and strengths that we frequently underestimate," the priest said as he gracefully rode off into the twilight.

Like my mother, the priest reminded me not to lose faith in the Lord and uphold the Christian faith as a moral guide. He stressed that correct behaviour is always an enrichment for the soul. He reminded me to pray daily, not only when I had problems.

15

GEORGETOWN

WITH FOUR PASSES IN O-level exams, I could join ranks with my pals Benny, Luke, and Winston in the country's bureaucracy. If I wanted. Now that opportunity came, the attraction was

gone––which was strange, I admitted, smiling and baffling my mates.

I had toyed with the idea of becoming a civil servant for years. It was a profession with social status, enough to strengthen one's ego and impress some class-conscious girls. I was bored with chasing after any girl who believed she was special. But that's another matter.

Entering the civil service to impress upper-class girls was ridiculous.

"What are your plans for the summer?" my father asked me. He delivered the question in his usual sly way, alluding to my current sleeping behaviour 'till ten, an hour before lunch.

I had no idea what I wanted from life or what life had in store for me this summer and beyond. My answer was that I was considering studying with a couple of friends and retaking maths. I added that I planned to find a summer job at a barrister's office.

My dad appeared to have accepted what I had told him, but I had no idea what he had up his sleeve. Usually, when there was no follow-up question from him or a concluding remark, he would return to the same subject, albeit from a different angle. It was a strategy to catch you off guard and discredit you. It was a way that some teachers used. I knew his way, as did my mother and siblings.

But I never got used to it. As far as I can remember, my father's deception troubled me in early and later puberty. After being caught off guard, I could not defend myself, stammered, and sounded foolish.

As an adult, I became aware of my tendency to blame myself in some social situations. I readily accepted the blame and apologised. That was after I had demonstrated hostility in the face of an unfair demand. I still wasn't sure whether my angry outburst had to do with childhood experiences—similarly, excessive guilt and taking on the role of a victim.

The suggestion for a summer job in a law firm came from a shy, if not close, friend. His name was Bertram, and he lived in the neighbourhood. We sang in the choir of Saint Philip's Anglican Church. His father worked as a sanitation inspector. Bertram stammered and joked about his sleepwalking and sleep-talking; he regularly received spankings from his mother, a headmistress in a Catholic primary school with a "fearful reputation."

All this and more fascinated me about Bertram. He was bright as hell and shining above the level of his classmates in primary and secondary school. At eleven, Bertram had won a scholarship to the best secondary school: Queen's College. He later won a national scholarship, allowing him to attend a top British university. I later learned Bertram had decided to study law at Oxbridge university. For years, I kept him in mind: he excelled academically despite his neurological trouble. Through friends, I later learned that Bertram became one of Britain's brilliant barristers, QC, and high court judge.

I took up Bertram's suggestion of "easily accessible, temporary employment" in a law firm, but it did not bear fruit. My father had the idea of working in his former department, and I subtly avoided it. Instead, I offered to deliver dresses my mother had sewn for customers. She had supported my initial need to take the summer break in strides, and, as always, I was grateful for her support.

I thought about the years of support from my mother. Did she spoil me? I'm not complaining because having both parents who were strict guardians would have been hell. I needed pampering, at least sometimes.

After the enormous impact and fatigue, I wanted a moment of zero stress this summer. I wanted a moratorium on a lifestyle of rules and regulations imposed by adults, particularly authoritarian personalities (which was another reason not to become a civil servant). I wanted to enjoy the freedom to pursue a teenager's happiness.

I might've had in mind Jim Stark (James Dean) in "Rebel Without a Cause."

When the family was short of bread for breakfast (a meal known as "morning tea"), I would go to my uncle Robert's bakery and receive free bread. My parents never wanted to eat bread from his bakery. I had no qualms about eating bread made by sweaty labour. I would pretend the fresh bread came from a machine bakery and pocket the cash.

To the surprise of my family (myself included), I found work at Uncle Robert's bakery. I remembered coming home with flour on my face and the smell of fresh bread and stale sweat.

My old man's beatings reappeared and then disappeared. To cope with the pain, I learned to contract my muscles. I also didn't scream in horror when I got hit. I realised my father was an unchangeable person. Irony, sarcasm, a roar, and a poisonous flow of silence were among the milder forms of aggression.

I imagined in some homes, loving support was seldom absent, where both parents had similar attitudes to upbringing. In some families, mothers would leave the punishment of their sons or daughters to their spouses. In families with missing fathers, mothers would dish out the beatings themselves.

NOW THAT A BEAUTIFUL summer was behind me, it was time to find a regular, decent job. I also had maths to retake. I only had time to review Sandra's notes and examples. Benny, Luke, and Winston were still willing to help me, but I was embarrassed to ask for their support again. So, of course, it was up to me. I started half-heartily with Sandra's math solutions, but in time I got bored.

Then my dad decided to surprise everyone in the family, which I regarded as an act of the gods, forcing him to be charitable to his younger son. I was due for a job interview as a junior reporter, or a trainee, in a daily newspaper's editorial department, where my dad once worked. The work included covering cases in the magistrate courts: pilfering, minor assaults, and traffic violations, like riding at night a bicycle without a light or riding on the pavement.

My father once worked as a foreman in the printing section but was made redundant long before his retirement. The reason for the redundancy remained inexplicable to me. I had it down to be either my father's drinking habit or his argumentative disposition. Of course, my mother rejected my insinuation. She gave my siblings and me the impression that it was due to the "bad blood" between the family's chief breadwinner and the newspaper's general manager.

After receiving severance or redundancy payment, Samuel Holmes became a self-employed watchman at government buildings and wealthy private homes. There was no fear about the family's money because Thomas and Faye both contributed.

The job interview seemed like a favour to my father from the newspaper's night editor, Mr Burgess. He was a massive guy with a hearty laugh as his bloated belly swayed. Samuel Holmes was exceedingly grateful during the job interview. My dad accompanied me, expressing his gratitude to the interviewee.

During the job interview, my father sat humbly. His demeanour was unusual, as if he had assumed another persona for the occasion, like a chameleon. The job interview was more like a discussion. I cast doubts about knowing the real Samuel Holmes.

At the interview, I pompously expressed appreciation for the opportunity I received. The burly fellow took my words with a graceful nod of the head.

In the end, Mr Burgess said he would first have to get clearance from the general manager, but there was nothing to worry about, just a routine matter.

The thought of becoming a journalist excited me. But I couldn't avoid being suspicious that my dad had some scheme––some form of chastisement to be delivered later.

Thomas once suppressed a chuckle during our father's insensitive remark about me. I was used to comments like that when my dad's consistency shone. He particularly loathed to portray himself as a "victim of circumstance," as he put it. The son of "humble parents" (his words), Samuel Holmes, didn't go beyond primary school. I reckoned he secretly harboured a grudge against people like doctors, lawyers, people with wealth, social prestige and the like. You could say he had mixed feelings about educated people.

When my dad and I arrived home, Samuel Holmes broke the news with a whiff of indifference to my mum. He made it appear like it was an easy accomplishment, and it probably was. My father stressed that he was still "someone with important connections" in his former workplace.

Mrs Holmes greeted the news. Looking at me, she uttered: "Your dad cares for you, Harry. Thank the Good Lord!" My mum exclaimed holy praise to allude to the prevailing notion among Christians that the Lord works in mysterious ways. Samuel Holmes didn't say a word, as if his initiative was enough.

It wasn't his wife's intention, for she was often willing to praise her husband or anyone else and the Lord in the same breath. She always reminded us of how important it is to thank our father for everything he had done for the family.

I later made a promise to my dad. I said, "I will do everything in my power to make you proud by being responsible, obedient, and diligent in the task at hand."

The movement may have been smooth, but it may have sounded like a piece of prose recited in primary school. My dad politely nodded as if moved by my performance. A flood of pride illuminated his face as he sipped a glass of rum and cola.

My father later offered to buy me a pair of trousers. He referred me to his tailor for the standard measurement procedure. He would select the material, most likely a gabardine fabric, which I wouldn't object not to ruining the show.

16

LONDON

WHILE HANGING OUT WITH the wrong group of friends, I adopted a laid-back approach to job hunting and mimicked their lifestyles. They might have mocked my longing to join the English multitude of workers.

I resumed my job search, and I must admit that I missed the comfortable lifestyle outside of the mainstream. It was a relief to sleep until noon after being awake until three a.m.

I restricted my job search to two weekly days and sent written job requests and applications I discovered in newspaper ads or through word of mouth from friends. Outlining the advantages and disadvantages of living in London, I wrote a letter to a friend or two back home.

I spent much of my free time reading became a form of bliss, a place where I could escape the here and now of discomfort––reading books in the Chelsea library. I'd occasionally buy a paperback or two from Smiths or Foyles. I was pleased to have rid myself of thievery.

Due to my unfortunate financial situation, I had to leave the three-bedroom apartment during the day. It was when you used gas heating or a fireplace. The heating devoured my meagre pocket money. The cold weather had become an issue in my life.

As a result, I frequently visited the Chelsea Library, the Student Centre, or a café. Other times after leaving the apartment, I felt warmer outside. I've never gotten used to English houses being too cold in the summer.

I once read that an Englishman's home was his castle. I'd always imagined such a house, complete with burning hearths, and there is nothing like first-hand knowledge. My hands and feet took the brunt of the damage. Most likely, moisture in the walls from a previous studio apartment and draughts from the windows and door. In stride, I sounded like an old geezer, and sometimes I was.

In England, I first became aware of my poor blood circulation. I'd gotten into the habit of walking with my hands in my pant pockets or jacket. I began to appreciate the warmth in the land of my birthplace and the tropical weather, which I used to take for granted. A few friendly English folks had asked me what brought me to a bleak and damp climate. I told them for *a better life*, but the hope was now showing signs of disappearing. I was too ashamed to return to Guyana and humiliate myself in front of family, friends, and adversaries. Admittedly, I would have used my mother's rescue plan. In addition to shame, it was my secret struggle or disagreement with my father.

The British had every reason to tell me to stop whining or return to my home country.

Gone was my insufficient desire to return to British Guiana (Guyana), "the land of hope and glory," because that country had never been my country. I never felt at home there––more like *an outsider*. Of course, I truly missed my friends, but many of them had gone to Canada or the US.

Furthermore, my life had changed, and there was no point in returning. I perceived myself as someone who needed a country and lacked national pride.

There were two three-bedroom apartments and some single rooms where I sought refuge from bad company. I rarely met tenants at any time of day except on weekends. Before coming to Britain, I longed for a life of anonymity. When I returned home from the Student Centre,

I occasionally crossed paths and met a young Asian woman in the early evening. She was probably my age, pretty but always without a smile and the same about a middle-aged couple with Asian features. They may or not be from the same country. I never saw the couple say hello to the young Asian woman. They never acknowledged my presence. Even when I once held the main door, they marched out without a sound or sign of appreciation. Thank you, I wanted to say. I resisted the temptation. That was when I learned not to take things personally, which wasn't easy, but developing a sarcastic demeanour came in handy.

One weekday around noon, as I walked down a flight of stairs where I lived, I noticed a white bloke, about thirty, dressed in green. He checked letters the postman had left on a table near a phone in the hallway. I had never seen him before and passed him as I made my way to the Student Centre for lunch.

When I returned that evening, Don and Leo informed me that someone had broken into the building's middle-aged Asian couple's flat. I mentioned my observation of a white man in green overalls going through the posts.

Another day, months later, when I entered the main door, my nostrils picked up a strong gas smell from somewhere on that floor. I knocked on every door on that floor and waited for an answer. I became increasingly concerned about the situation and dialled 911 from the hall.

With the main entrance door open, I stood at the entrance, on the street, waiting for the police to arrive. To my surprise, in about ten minutes, a vehicle with two plainclothes police officers appeared in a hurry but without the sound of sirens. They had contacted the landlord, for he, a stocky, quick-witted guy, soon showed up on foot. They could understand from where the gas came. Only the police and the landlord entered the room. Standing in the hallway, I curiously idled back to the entrance. I had nothing better to do with my time, and the cold wind didn't bother me.

A minute later, I heard a siren sound and noticed an ambulance. Two men in green uniforms hurried past me with a stretcher. They carried a woman in her early thirties out of the room a few minutes later. She appeared in slumber, with dishevelled brunette hair and her body covered with an ambulance blanket.

Don later told me it was a suicide attempt. I never again set eyes on the woman.

I REMEMBER REFLECTING on how society was only sometimes just. Because I've become aware of larger-scale inequality since moving to London, perhaps it was universal, or at least widespread in most countries.

My hometown had social and economic class differences and a divide between "the haves" and "the have-nots." I might have regarded it as the natural order of things at the time, with some succeeding and others failing. Religion's duality of good and evil may have influenced my outlook, self-image, and self-esteem. I don't recall blaming anyone for inequality. Politics was a subject that piqued my interest. Religion shaped my perspective on myself and the world by teaching me to help the poor and be kind to others. I first became concerned about widespread inequality in England.

Before moving to England, I assumed that English people were a unique breed, like the English in British Guiana (Guyana), only to discover that this was not the case. It was as if I had been clinging to a childhood fantasy all these years.

The English class system was complex, with upper (lower upper and upper), middle, working, and lower classes (maybe to which I belonged). I thought about the British class system and how it affects ethnicity, "persons of colour," and even (other) aliens in the UK.

In a society like Britain, where racism and racial discrimination are commonplace, I wondered if wealth and social standing serve as a shield. I imagined both made a difference, if not wholly, because racism, like magic, could appear anywhere.

Xenophobia and racism--both words have a semantic overlapping with *nativism,* which defines *favouring native inhabitants as opposed to immigrants*--seem to have existed since the beginning of time. God created Man and Woman, and His work was flawless.

The phenomenon has been around since the beginning of time. I recall learning that God created the world and all creatures, *great and small* and that His creation was once perfect. To paraphrase, one of my Sunday school teachers, Adam and Eve, messed things up by weaving a web of sin over human existence.

17

GEORGETOWN

I WAS JUST OVER NINETEEN when I started my first decent job, which I was surprised to get. I wasn't sure if Mr Burgess, the night editor, had been honest with my father and me. I thought about my father's need to impress his family. Because he believed he was still a man of influence in his former workplace, which struck me as ironic given that he got fired. At the end of the interview, I was secretly cynical that the editor-in-chief had to settle the matter with Davenport's managing director, who had fired my father. Mr Burgess' words sounded suspicious, but I kept them to myself and didn't even want to tell my mother. I expected time to reward my cynicism, but I was wrong, which was good for both him and me.

The first few days, I awoke at 7 a.m., far from my low mood at such early hours. It felt like I was at a crossroads in my life. I despised the sound of the morning alarm clock during my school years because it constantly interrupted my peaceful slumber. Some school days were difficult for me. On Saturdays, I despised my household chores. On my knees, I polished the living room floor while washing my father's large-framed bicycle and my mother's. I also delivered a few dresses she had made for customers during lunchtime in the sweltering heat. Not to mention Sundays, when Mass begins at eight a.m.

My eagerness to get up and go to work included the following:

1. Dressing in a white shirt and blue tie.
2. Dark blue trousers (a gift from my father).
3. Black socks.
4. Shiny black shoes.

I cycled for twenty minutes to the city's heart. I saw girls and boys dressed in school uniforms. Men and women dressed smartly, including me, manual workers already working, and the unemployed and underemployed, who most likely ran errands or were idle daily. Two friends occasionally joined me on my way to work.

At work, colleagues introduced themselves. I took a short tour of the linotype and compositing departments to gain an understanding of interconnected processes and routines. My tasks included editing a copy of my article written by the linotypist. In the beginning, I accompanied a full-fledged reporter who taught me the ropes of the trade. My department included a few young or older women and more men than women.

My attention strayed to a handsome young woman dressed smartly in a cream blouse and a flared maroon skirt working in the bookbindery where my mother had previously worked. I vowed to concentrate on the tasks ahead, wanting to reassure my parents about my responsible demeanour.

My enthusiasm for work began to wane around the fourth or fifth month. I was dissatisfied with my salary, which was pitiful. I would make light of it with close friends. The compensation did not give me the means to go on dates, pay for housing at home (my father's idea), or buy things in cash, but rather in monthly instalments.

In addition, my mother insisted that I set aside a small sum each month for unforeseen circumstances. My financial situation was not one of which I was particularly proud.

The situation had deteriorated. On a salary like mine, how should I assume the role of a responsible citizen? I'd reflect on that time a year or more later, burdened by immaturity.

After hearing my complaint, my mum advised me to save first and buy later, only spending a little of my income on clothes. She urged me to take a healthy attitude toward money, which showed much responsibility. She stressed that I should allow Christian moral values to guide me. Only sometimes did my mother understand me. My focus went away from the dining table, where my mother was stitching. My gaze drifted, and I spotted a small swarm of ants battling with breadcrumbs on their way somewhere.

Then I heard my mum shout, "Oh, no, the devil's a busy beast."

The bobbin thread on the sewing machine had run out.

After a few years, I'd recognise the wisdom of saving a small portion of my monthly salary and avoiding impulsive purchases on credit.

I've always tried to obey my mother and keep my rudeness to a minimum. She understood I was ignoring her financial advice and saw it as a symptom of immaturity, a problem of youth. Sandra was always frugal with her money and a good saver.

My tasks were straightforward, and boredom set in. I wanted more significant assignments now but needed the experience to do them. It was not common practice to use the try-and-error method.

At this game stage, concise and medium-sized articles fit my expertise. They were easy to write; simple procedures became dull over time, so my thoughts drifted. I occasionally tried to add some spice to my pieces.

My mentor, Charlie Griffith, however, dismissed it. A tough old bugger, I thought, who appeared to be in the same league as my father in terms of humourlessness. He was a total jerk.

He delivered a brief sermon: "Holmes junior, please rid yourself of all such temptations! Leave it to writers of fiction and people in the entertaining or advertising business," Mr Griffith had squeaked. "But not in this business. Please show respect for authentic human misfortunes and sufferings."

I readily complied with his demands, dispensing with my propensity for cynical humour and sticking to the facts of the case. I felt "like a cent ice" (in Guyanese parlance, for feeling humiliated). I recall how the scolding tormented me, taking pleasure, as it were, in mocking my penchant for cynical humour.

I dislike persons who claim to have at their disposal knowledge and facts that are irrefutable – black-and-white, denying grey. Maybe I'm of a similar disposition, and my dislike is a projection. I try to remember that *being right is primarily a matter of explanation* to reproduce the words of a dramatist.

Once, when my mood was low, I told my mother about boredom at work and insisted she should not say a word to my father. I explained that my enthusiasm for the job had waned. I suspected it was due to my impulsive attitude to becoming a respected citizen.

I confessed it was all childish. But the excitement was gone, as in early and later childhood moments, when positive feelings ceased. Positive emotions continued to leave me high and dry – perhaps like a hangover after a drinking session.

In a confessional mood, I indulged in spiritual self-flagellation. I lacked judgment and responsibility and needed help taking life seriously. My mum had always been concerned about my emotional immaturity, but she remained supportive. She would encourage me to pray to "God the Father, the Son and the Holy Ghost" for guidance and strength. My mother was steadfast in her belief that "all the children of God have a meaning in life." Faith played a central role in searching for happiness and love.

Later in life, I realised I had placed unrealistic expectations on my parents. I had no idea at the time, not while I was still green. It was as if I had been stuck in the growth cycle when a child thought his parents were divine.

How can you help others in a significant way without their involvement? I would learn parents can do so much, but not everything, by witnessing close friends' challenges in their parental roles.

I was grateful for the support my mother gave me. At times, her word was final in minor matters, but she was no match regarding dominance in the family. My mother had moral strength, but her actions became restrained as if she didn't want to undermine her husband's role. Her Christian faith might have been the influential force instead of her character. I had once asked my three aunts about what their eldest sister was like before her marriage. They indicated a slight change in my mum's personality, but that was all. Perhaps they avoided the attempt to relate more.

My mother had always encouraged me to be patient and pray for strength and guidance from the Almighty Lord. Her words temporarily comforted me. Meanwhile, I wanted a compassionate, understanding, and supportive father. Perhaps it was the gods' will: father and mother should have their respective roles, although both should be supportive.

It was unfortunate because my good friend Lucky (Lee) had a father to whom he could confide and seek fatherly advice. My life lacked a proper father-son relationship: it was one-sided. I had no other option but to be obstinate, defiant, and absent-minded.

My siblings, mother and I were regular churchgoers, and I was a chorister. My religious beliefs did not match those of my mother. The love of God had been instilled in me, while the fear of God's wrath had driven it. Despite my high regard for the Lord, I struggled in my adolescent years to understand the Lord's supreme power as opposed to Satan's. Reverend Batty, our Methodist priest, presented it at Sunday Mass. I wanted to believe that the devil had no chance against the Lord.

I chastised myself for being a frail vessel. I would also accuse Adam and Eve of making things difficult for themselves.

What was I to do? "Have faith in the Lord," my mother said. "What is there to do, son, but to seek a decent life under the guidance of the Lord?"

Nothing made sense, so my mind had yet to decide what I wanted. Perhaps it was God's punishment. I told my mother that I desired happiness and joy through material possessions, a pleasant social life, and a lot of fun, friends and girlfriends. My mother reminded me that the Christian life was about giving rather than wanting and resisting Satan's false pearls and fleeting riches.

My mother was speaking to me in the same tone as my father. Her loyalty seemed to shift. I was stunned, hurt, and perplexed. So, what triggered her unexpected change of heart? I remained baffled.

Later, I decided that telling her about my problems was childish. I reasoned that I needed to learn to bear my burdens and let go of Mommy's boy tendencies. My parents and I came from different worlds. If I lived at home, I would be at their disposal.

Sandra was highly fortunate, was successful in school, happy at work, and appeared to be in love. Like her mother, she never mentioned her problems. Her boyfriend, Mark, was charming and attractive, but I didn't believe him. Sandra marrying him wouldn't surprise me in the least.

What was the point of my existence? I didn't have any real answers. In retrospect, I vehemently opposed everything. Though I continue to deny it, I have not changed much, if at all. My mind became bombarded with questions. My fascination with nature evolved into what it means to be a human and the meaning of life. Was the purpose of my life? I had no real answers. I was defiant against every bloody thing.

18

LONDON

THE ARRIVAL OF AN ENGLISH summer meant that the days became brighter and sunnier, with a few clouds and a bright blue sky. I stopped at a red light for pedestrians as vehicles and one or more cyclists flew by. The first thing I noticed about cyclists in London was that they were a brave bunch. The red light was visible for a more extended period than usual. When it finally turned green, I dashed over, my hands in my coat pockets. Will I be able to beat the Tube today? It had become a habit, but I eventually learned to make better decisions. At some stations, the risk of being caught red-handed was high, which was not on my wish list.

I was standing at the station's entrance. The newspaper vendor, an English bloke, about sixty and probably an ex-soldier, in rumpled camouflage trousers and a worn-out black lumber jacket, appeared troubled by a few mischievous kids. They pelted each other with pebbles. One hit the newspaper vendor on the mouth because his left hand rested as if in pain.

"Hey, you lot! You hit me with something! *Ain't* you lot in school? Runoff, you bugger!" He said it out loud with a frown on his face.

The vendor tried to catch one of the youngsters, mostly 11 years old, but they laughed and ran off, chuckling. I stood there, the difference in the old guy's discomfort, remembering my wayward ways as a kid and adults as the enemy. These playful days were some of the highlights of my schooldays, aside from my menacing school assignments.

The station looked good. The cashier chatted with someone, and the ticket collector was missing. I sped up, pretended to be rushed, and knitted my brow to show my urgency. Reaching the escalator, descending, and losing sight of the ticket booth or ticket collector was a joy.

Taking the risk was indeed foolish.

19

GEORGETOWN

I WAS SURPRISED TO have a job still when I was nineteen. I wouldn't say I liked it, but I made the best of it. Perhaps I acted masochistically. I suffered in silence, accepting the present moment and ignoring my dissatisfaction in whatever form it took, primarily through daydreams, which I indulged in frequently as a child and teenager. I began to regard my job as a means of subsistence. My attitude towards money shifted. Despite my initial discontent, my mother's advice reached me. She was great at saving money, and I admired her practicality in situations where I later realised how impractical I was.

I periodically rewarded myself with a rum store (bar) visit after work with my colleagues. I spoke light-heartedly about things in general over a glass or two. After an hour, boredom arose, and I apologised and departed. Conversation with work colleagues didn't feel the same as with my mates. I rarely talked about my personal life at work.

I recall a strange dream. I wanted to talk about it with someone other than my mother, Sandra, or close friends. Some people routinely told strangers about their personal lives, but I kept mine to myself. I didn't expect anyone to understand my bizarre dreams. Some dreams made little or no sense at all. Essentially the goal was for me to be part of a glorified group of socialites, charismatic brothers and sisters of a light skin tone. Each carried placards displaying family social status, prestige, and a privilege that the group flaunted. My banner was devoid of glamour. There was no glamour on my flag. I had nothing to brag about, nothing to be proud of, nothing to match the glorified group of quadroons.

My mother shook me: "It's time to get up, Harry! You spoke in your sleep. What were you dreaming?"

How could I explain to my mother that my dream represented the idea that I wasn't proud of who I was?

I had other strange dreams, but this one kept coming back. Its memory came and went in waves, as did thoughts about who I was or pretended to be.

I knew that I could come across as vain at times. One of my co-workers, Willow Walters (baby Huey, to close pals), first made me aware of my attitude. It was as if I, a tar baby, had nothing to be vain about, not even a morsel of false vanity. I recalled shrugging aside the comment.

Years later, when I was irritated and allowed myself to become arrogant, Willow's remark reappeared. When my humility returned, I felt mortified. My conceitedness usually showed its ugly countenance in the company of unfriendly strangers or workmates with a condescending attitude toward me. It aggravated my inferiority complex. My vanity had become a shield, a fortress, in defence of my fragile self-image and self-esteem.

20

LONDON

SUDDENLY, I HAD A STRANGE feeling. At first, I didn't understand why the symptoms were so severe. I remember feeling guilty while "beating the Tube," but I wouldn't attribute it to this or anything else. Even in the safety of my lodging, this sensation came over me, albeit milder and for no apparent reason: pulsating heartbeat, heavy breathing, dizziness, and slight nausea. And diffuse fear.

The state lasted only a few minutes, though it felt much longer before things calmed down, and I regained a sense of serenity, despite feeling exhausted and warm. What the hell was that? My inner voice asked.

I have no idea what happened to me. Was it a prelude to madness? When I was about seven, I remembered my maternal Grandpa Adam "going off his head." My mother had only said a few words, as if that would suffice for someone my age. I overlooked Grandpa Adam's insanity, only his absence and that he had been taken to a place "to get well."

Years later, I learned from my mother again about Grandpa's nervous breakdown, which occurred out of the blue, as it were. Perhaps it resulted from much stress, a nervous disposition, or something else. The thought of losing my bearings in a whirlpool of psychological chaos would resurface and fill me with dread.

I wanted to see my GP, but the ambivalence got the best of me. I was terrified of being referred to a mental institution. I avoided telling anyone about my nervous state. Alcohol became a substitute, which was beneficial. However, there was always a risk of over-consuming alcohol to soothe one's nerves.

I decided to pay the full fare on the Tube, which didn't take too long to arrive. I took a seat. There would be only three stops. There weren't many commuters: some wore formal attire, while others wore casual clothing. Of course, I assumed the latter was unemployed. Unlike in my hometown, it wasn't a reliable way to judge strangers in London.

I jerked my right hand into the breast pocket of my overcoat, thinking I'd forgotten to take my Insurance Card. But there was no reason for me to worry. It was a false alarm, a catastrophic thought, no doubt.

A passenger got up and exited. He had either left or forgotten a copy of the Daily Mirror. The headline reads STRIKE HITS CAR INDUSTRY. In another headline: UNEMPLOYMENT FIGURES DOWN. I considered going after the newspapers but sensed my actions would appear stingy. I decided to wait until it was time to disembark. The Tube squealed as it came to a halt. I retrieved the newspaper, the doors slid open, and five of us stepped onto the platform.

The smartly dressed male passengers arrived at the Labour Exchange. The time on the wall was 10.20 a.m. My wristwatch was ten minutes late, as is typical of low-cost watches.

I joined a medium-sized queue. We were a mixed lot: young, middle-aged, and older people, some unkempt, sitting or standing or strolling around, rolling cigarettes (there were "no smoking" signs, at least as far as I recalled), chatting or complaining, or quietly awaiting their turn—the odour of stale sweat, possibly from dirty clothes or an unwashed body. I felt uneasy and must have appeared restless, exhaling through my mouth. I was hypersensitive to smells.

The Labour Exchange was where I wanted to spend little time and be gone. I might have signalled my discomfort with an exaggerated facial and bodily expression--which looked sufficient to warrant a question from someone:

"Have a problem, mate? You look distressed." A chorus of laughter erupted.

"A bit of an allergic discomfort, no more," I mumbled without directly facing whoever raised the question.

Should I have expressed my disdain for the flock? My fate was the same as theirs; life had put us in the same boat.

My line came to a halt. A middle-aged man (Irish, by his brogue) questioned why they reduced his weekly benefit to the attending official. I continued reading the Daily Mirror and breathing through my mouth, diverting my attention from the argument ahead. I soon discovered that the newspaper was two days old.

When it was my turn, the clerk took my card and leafed through cabinet files. The search was taking some time. I've never seen the clerk before; he could be new.

"I cannot locate your file, Mr Holmes," the official said when he returned. "Have you been here recently?" What a brilliant question from a civil servant, I thought. I was overcome with embarrassment and irritation and despised drawing attention to myself. I heard myself say: "That's a strange thing to ask. Is there no one to assist you?" My embarrassment had faded, leaving the irritation to fend for me. Perhaps prompted by my remark, the clerk hurried off. He was conversing with an older colleague. They both went to the same file cabinet, and after a quick search, the younger man returned with my file.

"I apologise for the inconvenience, Mr Holmes," the younger clerk said, trying to smile.

In turn, I uttered it was ok--which was deceitful. I was eager to claim my dole and leave that dreadful environment.

After receiving my weekly allowance request, I had to join another queue at the checkout. After being distracted by the low humming sound of "Ole Man River," I felt like I were in the company of an unpleasant individual.

The individual was a white male, of medium height and a wiry build, with black, unkempt hair and a half beard, and a dishevelled appearance. He stood a few feet away from my queue. He looked like a street performer, judging from his clothing. He locked his gaze on mine for a moment. This white stranger busted into the song "Bojangles" (the lyrics delivered with a foreign accent, perhaps from Eastern Europe) and did a rendition of a Zulu War dance or another. Laughter erupted, and I sensed all eyes on me. I felt, as though by telepathy, the expectation to participate in whatever way I could. Later, I wondered if I missed the cheerfulness or the tribute to two outstanding black performers.

My blackness felt targeted. I struggled to keep myself together as humiliation gripped me. It was as if the spectacle had little or nothing to do with Harry Holmes. It could well have been a satirical piece performed by a street entertainer, possibly addicted to the "spotlight" or looking for a quick buck––or even a lunatic.

After collecting my meagre though badly needed weekly benefit, I quickly fled, away from the horrific, into a labyrinth of obscurity and a never-ending conundrum.

Later, I would strive to rationalise the incident to ease the emotional pain. I considered it an act of no significance, which was my way of putting the matter into a distant memory.

As my time in London progressed, I became more sensitive to being judged based on my skin colour or race. I wanted to be treated as an individual, not as a collective member of something, and to avoid stereotyping. Of course, it was something over which I had no control.

The gods or something else punished me even more. Attending the Labour Exchange was still a source of embarrassment.

21

GEORGETOWN

USUALLY, I WOULD GO straight home after work to nap, shower, and have dinner. I would cycle to a friend's house, where other friends had gathered. Or I'd loiter in my neighbourhood corner with members of the working class (as my father would have it), chatting and laughing about various topics. Mostly about comic moments, like misadventures, either sexual or non-sexual.

Other times it was about sporting events, dramatic films from the 1940s or current films. I would attend a basketball game or a soft-shoe soccer match at the Parade Ground. Or I would visit a nine o'clock movie at Astor, Empire, Globe, or Plaza cinema with friends.

I partied on Fridays since I couldn't stay out too late on Saturdays and Sundays following early Mass. On Fridays or Saturday afternoons, I would attempt to date a girlfriend.

Nonetheless, life in Georgetown became monotonous and provincial. Probably over time, with many American and British films I'd seen, the talk of opportunities overseas by acquaintances who probably had relatives or friends abroad. All of this might have contributed to my sulky unhappiness in Guyana. Something seemed to be missing from my life. Sometimes I got bored with things I once liked. Parental control might have been part of it. I began to fantasise about living in another country that might offer more or something different, inspiring me to add significance and meaning to my life. Also, one gave me enough space from parental rules and influences: I needed to get by and stand on my own two feet.

It was crucial to know that my mother loved me. On the other hand, my father convinced me he had no feelings for me, even though my desire to be loved was probably proof of my affection. I, for one, didn't think it showed how vain I was.

I became aware of the random events in my life. It wasn't Christian-like. By the quirk of fate, I could've been born in any country or not at all.

MY LOVE LIFE WAS STILL not bringing me much joy. It didn't go like in American love movies, which presented a different reality and reminded me of what I was missing. There were romantic stories on the celluloid screen that seemed far-fetched. However, there were realistic stories with happy endings. Beyond that, I was part of the problem: I was all talk and no action, captivated by physical attractiveness rather than content.

I dated attractive girls who just saw me as a friend, yet the dates impressed my buddies and boosted my ego. It was something I exploited to the point of frustration. Conversations on such dates frequently revolved around broken romance or unrequited love as shown in films or as experienced in real life. I rarely went out with girls who weren't both pretty and classy, even if the potential of a romantic relationship did not exist. Lovemaking wasn't crucial to my schedule. I would subsequently scold myself for that era of folly and wasted possibilities that may have helped me build my intimate knowledge and skills.

After the movie "Tea and Sympathy", at age sixteen, I wanted to have an intimate relationship with an older woman. Maybe she could teach me the A-B-C of erotic love. Despite some near attempts, I never got "lucky" with an older woman. For one thing, the women I was interested in lived too close to my house, and they even knew my parents.

During my senior year in high school, I stopped mimicking some American actors' romantic styles. I sought less advice from older male friends in the neighbourhood, which was never helpful. Instead, I started putting theories I'd read in books into practice.

In retrospect, my lack of experience may have protected me from the traps of promiscuity and other vices.

AFTER OVERSLEEPING, I hurriedly rode my bike to a rendezvous with friends one evening. In a hurry, I foolishly attempted to adjust the front fender while my eyes were forward, and my left hand dared to do so. Then my hand became trapped between the spokes of the front wheel. I was yanked forward, hit the upper lip of the bike's left-side handlebar and somersaulted onto the road.

I later considered myself fortunate that the accident did not occur on a major road. I was lucky. The injury was minor: a cut on the left side of my upper lip that didn't require stitches but left a scar. I could have sustained a shoulder fracture or head injury from the fall. I had to have three upper front teeth extracted a few years later because their roots got damaged in the accident.

22

LONDON

TWO WEEKS LATER, ONE cold and windy Friday morning in autumn.

"Please sign here, Mr Holmes," said the clerk at the Labour Exchange, who seemed pleased with himself. I signed an unfamiliar yellow form.

"That will be all, Mr Holmes," the clerk said after inspecting my signature and returning my insurance card.

My heartbeat increased. I stared at the clerk, clearing my throat. "Hmm! What about my claim?" It was the slip of paper I took to the cashier. Temporarily I lost my speech. At the back of the line, I heard somebody say: "Get on with it, mate! You don't have all day!"

Surprisingly, the voice and protest did not bother me, as if there was no time for it. Meanwhile, the official, a young man with knitted eyebrows and his mouth agape, left, ostensibly in search of my claim.

He came back. "I haven't located your claim, I'm afraid," the young official said. "Perhaps there's a misunderstanding or --"

"Or what, what do you mean?" I interrupted. A stutter occasionally affected my speech, usually when I was confused and insecure, but rarely when I was angry. "There hadn't previously been any hindrance to my claim. What's going on?"

I had to wait for another clerk to investigate the matter.

My mind was in full swing as I sat patiently waiting for them to resolve the matter. It wasn't my day, I thought, feeling as though I was suffering at the hands of a white-collar novice. I wasn't good at suffering fools gladly. I wondered *what had happened to the slip. Had I missed something mailed to me or was it governmental incompetence?*

Civil servants remained my adversaries. I've never had much faith in them. Nevertheless, why would intelligent folks like my darling sister Sandra, Faye, and some of my friends and cousins, Sam, become civil servants in God's name?

In retrospect, I never understood why I disliked civil servants who had a right to earn a living. Some of my feelings are like that: they obstruct my ability to think clearly.

Years later, the bank clerks and insurance regulators tasted my spleen.

"Mr Harry Holmes?" came from the voice of another much older official.

"Finally," I said. "Yes, that's me!" My angry mood had now taken a back seat, allowing politeness to shine through.

"Please come with me."

I followed him into a cubicle, where I sat in front of a desk as he sat opposite me.

"Are you still living at the same address, Mr Holmes?"

"Yes, that's the one I submitted a few weeks ago."

"How is the job search going?"

"Constantly," I smiled. "Enough to make me lose my mind! I've letters of rejection to substantiate my answer––all kept in a file."

The official held a stone face. I got the message: the situation warranted seriousness, no laughing matter, a colony of zombies - civil servants!

"We sent a letter to your current address."

"Wait, letter, what letter?" A rush of insolence popped out.

"It didn't reach your attention, apparently," said the official.

"It should have. Mail deliveries aren't 100 per cent reliable. I check for mail regularly." My irritation had returned.

The male official looked at me as if he was ready to give me a piece of his mind.

He said, "There've been questions in your file concerning the difficulty you're experiencing in obtaining a job. I understand you once worked as a journalist. You haven't had any luck there either?"

"It wasn't a question of failing," I said, with pinched brows. "I considered it a waste of time because I wasn't a qualified journalist in that far-flung British colony in South America. The standards for job qualification are higher in Britain."

"That is correct, and I understand," the official said. "Let me be straight with you, Mr Holmes. We suspended your benefits, subject to a new appraisal. A visit to your current address. Here's a date for an upcoming visit." His outstretched arm placed a sheet of paper on my side of the table.

I took up the sheet of paper, folded it, and stuffed it into the inside pocket of my black jacket. The official and I stood up and went our ways.

23

GEORGETOWN

ONCE, I ACCOMPANIED a friend, Buddy, to locate a supposedly attractive lady of lustful bliss. It was Christmas Eve. He couldn't possibly expect Santa to be a procurer of such pleasure. I was intrigued by the encounter and fantasised about "ladies of the night," but they only appeared in my dreams. It was my way of showing him moral support by tagging along.

Buddy and I arrived on Main Street, a downtown capital business district of Georgetown. The street carried a beautiful avenue, lined with parallel rows of trees, their base and lower trunks painted in white, and grass on each side along an asphalt aisle—a crowded area with last-minute buyers and window shoppers, mostly youths in small groups and adults. Carols blared from speakers on building tops, mostly from shops and stores. There was a high-end hotel nearby where some guests and visitors mingled at its entrance, and a couple alighting from or entering Bookers' taxis.

Our gaze roved the area as we strolled along, looking for a tall, elegantly dressed, and handsome light-brown-skinned woman walking down the lovely avenue. Buddy stated that she carried herself gracefully and that recognising her would be simple. He sounded enthralled and ecstatic. Buddy claimed, "the lady hails from Barbados." I reckoned that he could have heard this from someone familiar with ladies of the night.

So, Buddy and I set out on Main Street grand avenue to find her. As we patrolled there, we met a wave of pedestrians coming and going. There were such ladies in the area, frolicking with each other. Some men approached them discreetly, engaging in a brief discourse or whatever.

But Buddy had not seen any sign of this remarkable lady of the night so far.

"What time is it?" I asked.

"Almost ten," Buddy said, frowning as he looked at his watch.

"Perhaps she's running late or something," I said, remaining diligent and hopeful in my search.

"That's possible, but other women in the business are already out."

Nonetheless, at eleven o'clock, and much to Buddy's displeasure, his lovely lady was nowhere to be found. I struggled to maintain my optimism. I held on to a vision of her from Buddy's description as if it were in flesh and blood.

"Are you willing to pay the price she demands? I asked.

"I don't know, Harry," Buddy remarked while stuffing both hands into the front pockets of his Levi's blue trousers as if defying himself.

"I have $10. I could lend you $5."

"I have $50. I reckon the lady in question is no cheap dame," he said.

"Man, that's a lot of money. Did you rob the Canadian Bank across the street?"

"From savings and a load from my father," he said, his gaze on the lookout.

"So, you're dead on sleeping with the Barbadian beauty," I said.

"Nothing to laugh about or witty remarks, Harry! For crying out loud, I need to get laid!"

"Ok. Ok. Why don't you let me set you up with one of those no-beating-about-the-bush girls with whom I flirt but have no desire to bed?"

"No, no! None of them! Not my speed!" Buddy said. "I'm looking for a lady who exudes class."

"The illusion of it, you mean," I said. "Indeed! It's your prerogative."

"Call it what you will, Harry. I know a classy courtesan when I see one."

"Ok. But that's a heavy price to pay to do it, a brief duration of erotic pleasure."

Finally, I said under my breath: there was no sign of a Barbadian beauty most likely lost in the arms of some wealthy lover. Buddy's dissatisfaction was palpable.

"Perhaps the holiday season isn't the best time for ordinary people like us, or she's probably home for Christmas," I said. Even courtesans, I'm sure, have someone special lurking in the shadows. After the holidays, you can always try your luck again. If you're lucky, the low season will likely result in a lower price!"

Buddy shrugged, his shoulders coming up to his ears and his gaze fixed on a cloudy sky and a sliver moon.

I wondered what he was thinking. My banter was of no comfort. I didn't consider it the end of the world, but he might've been experiencing a mood change, possibly one gloomy one. It was too easy to misjudge or understand others, to see things through one's prejudices. I propose that he and I go for a drink and wish each other a Merry Christmas while he ignores the absence of bodily pleasure."

"All right, but only for a little while," Buddy said, nodding. "Not following through on my plan ruined my Christmas Eve." I promised to assist my mother in the preparation of a cake."

I said, "So, it's that bad, eh? I misjudged your situation. There is rarely a guarantee for getting things right all the time, especially intimacy. Doing it with your Barbadian beauty might not have satisfied your heart's desire."

I spoke too much. I should have made room for silence. I might reflect on the situation later and lament my inability to console anyone.

"I know, I know," Buddy said after a brief pause. I'm not a nincompoop! It's all conjecture at our age. Let's save this discussion for our adult years, Harry."

"That's sensible! Forget 'bout my chattering! Your point taken!"

He nodded and looked at me.

"Perhaps I'd go home too and surprise my mum. I don't expect my dad to be home until the wee hours of the morning." I laughed.

"My father is the same way," Buddy chuckled. "Let's go get a drink!"

We rode our bikes for ten minutes to the nightclub. Mammy's was on Regent Street.

I once visited there with friends to compete in a drinking contest. The competition was to see how well we could hold our drinks. I rode my pushbike to my aunties' house to spend the night and vomit before knocking on their door. I didn't want my mother and father to see me in this state.

Buddy and I made our way to Mammy's Nightclub. I bought him a beer, and we sat at the bar. My gaze wandered around the room, and my mind assessed the night's young but mostly middle-aged ladies.

Two smiling women soon approached us, and we ended up at their table. My lady was Portuguese, young, sensual, medium height, slender, and dressed to kill. Her features reminded me of a Hollywood actress or a model from Sandra's Vogue magazine. She introduced herself as Marylou. The other woman was older and of East Indian and African descent (a *dougla* which wasn't offensive). She approached Buddy. Soon it became apparent that Buddy's attention drew elsewhere: his stare fixed on Marylou. His face was bright and cheerful, like a Christmas tree.

As a favour to him, I began chatting up the dougla woman in her forties; my inner voice now echoed the opportunity to do it with an older woman. Her name was Josephine. I thought of Napoleon Bonaparte's true love Joséphine de Beauharnais, although there was no resemblance beyond the name and vocation.

Buddy winked at me. I was delighted for him. The mood for adventure had descended upon my mate and me. My time had arrived to do it with a lady of the night and older. I smiled to myself.

Hurriedly, Buddy and I rushed through our beer before escorting the ladies to separate rooms.

The "damage" (price) was $5 in local currency. I was elated and prepared for what I had to do.

Soon, the *dougla* woman turned out to be a mistake. Joséphine had kept reminding me to "hurry up," as if to drive home the point. I assumed it was a time-limited affair or her way of making a quick buck from an exploit.

So, I didn't relish the moment; I felt cheated; my act was incomplete. I got dressed and walked out, disgusted, muttering: "What a waste of time and money!" My long-held desire to date a mature woman had turned into a nightmare. I felt cheated. I promised myself I wouldn't fall into such a trap again.

Buddy, on the other hand, had no complaints. He said he had told Marylou it was his first time, and she complimented his performance. He was overjoyed, and I tried to appear cheerful for his sake. I took solace in my friend being "off the shelf," and I allowed myself to be glad on his behalf.

It took me a while to fall asleep after entering my bed after midnight, with malicious whispers and mental echoes of condemnation tormenting me. As I awoke, the whispering and echoing reappeared, keeping 'me company' on Christmas Day.

24

LONDON

THE LABOUR EXCHANGE official was going to inspect my lodging on Tuesday, but I spent the entire morning waiting. My mood was down because I hadn't gotten a good night's sleep. The night before, Don and Leo wished me good luck. I tried listening to some of Don's Reader's Digest compilation of classical music to relax my mood, but the feeling remained the same. So, I decided to listen to the Dave Brubeck Quartet and the Ahmad Jamal Trio, which helped lift my mood. I even was able to take a nap.

Then, just before noon, I heard the main doorbell ring. The official presented her name (Mrs Fiona Campbell) as we greeted each other. She apologised for the delay. Such visits took place before midday, but I'm not sure. I led the way up a flight of stairs. The official complained of workload and congestion. I imagined *she was probably a wife and mother of three children and had much work in the office and at home*. I asked her whether she was from London.

"Oh no," she said, "I was born in Glasgow, Scotland."

Mrs Campbell, the official, said, after a brief tour of my room and the rest of the apartment, "It's a nice flat." I informed her that I pay £4 per week in rent and that the flat only had two other occupants.

The official sympathised with my job search and social/personal issues.

My benefits continued, but so did my job search. I still had to deal with the unpredictable peaks and valleys of anxious moods.

I went to see my doctor, who was sympathetic. Dr Mary Rogers was originally from Cardiff, Wales. My fear of being committed to a psychiatric facility was unfounded. I was given a preliminary diagnosis of generalised anxiety and was prescribed medication before an impending attack.

After some time, the drug seemed to help. Dr Rogers advised me to phase out the medication and start with deep-breathing exercises as directed.

During the consultation, she asked me what I was doing or thinking before an attack. After some thought, I answered that I couldn't remember or that it wasn't anything special. She said I should try to capture the moment before each attack and stop it. It was a way to neutralise my negative thoughts, which sometimes amplified the attack.

At first, her advice sounded odd, but it made sense to me with time.

Dr Rogers thought I had mild depression but no concern for alarm or medication. She arrived at this conclusion after asking me some specific questions. I recall her telling me not to limit myself to negative thoughts. Her advice came after I mentioned a change in my life after entering secondary school: the demand from others and myself around fifteen. I was under tremendous pressure, both at school and at home.

During Mrs Campbell's home visit, I mentioned my GP's advice. Mrs Campbell was a mother of two teenage boys and said she understood what I was going through. I appreciated the brief conversation at the end of the visit.

I had not written to my mum about my anxiety, my problem at the Labour Exchange, or my other struggle to obtain work. I wanted to protect her from worrying. I missed her, and the impulse entered me to tell my mum I wanted to come home. Whenever I got a fever from a bad cold, I longed for my mother, a child's first love, some say, and tears fell.

But the days of being Mommy's boy were over. I was now a man and not a child. When I was five or six years old, I remembered yearning to be an adult, to live a free life, and to make something of myself.

I hadn't told my Guyanese friends about my fear or difficulty finding work. It's not something you shout from the rooftops.

I took the advice to try to see the bright side of things. Looking on the bright side was a positive attitude, and my mother used to say when things were bad for her or her family—such optimism is a part of the Christian faith.

My situation in England had changed drastically compared to my life in Guyana. I tried not to think of it as the end of the world. I'd taken my GP's advice: I should shield my mind from the constant flow of negative thoughts and try to be cheerful and outward-looking. I should socialise and spend less time thinking about my problems, for life was for living, and that lousy luck rarely lasted forever.

There's a saying that many people unnecessarily spend much of their lives worrying. Was I such a person? Was my life cycle changing for the worse? With my struggle with alcohol and anxiety, I began to understand the importance of my mother's approach to life problems: we must face them as best we can.

25

GEORGETOWN

I WASN'T THE ONLY ONE who thought about leaving Guyana. Friends and strangers expressed an interest in emigrating or studying abroad. I wanted to live in a different country and broaden my perspective on life. I tried to avoid the risk of marrying or fathering several children by mistake, all customs and practices in human existence. I was afraid of tying myself too quickly and blowing my dreams to the wind.

Yes, I was terrified of losing control so early in my life - just like that! I noticed a pattern of local men pulled in this direction and then trapped in quicksand. They were primarily men on meagre income or temporary workers who had seen their hopes for a better future die. I didn't want to give up my hopes of self-actualisation and a better future.

Living in big cities like New York, Paris and London had always appealed to me: glamour, romance, and even anonymity. Probably Hollywood left an impression on me and inspired my youth imagination to be drawn to the spectacular side of things and life.

The freedom from parental influence undoubtedly influenced the desire to travel abroad. My siblings and I lived at home, as was customary until you married or moved abroad. I worked and contributed to household expenses. But my father denied me certain privileges: I couldn't come home late at night, smoke, or drink alcohol at home. Thomas received those privileges.

At that time, I concluded that my father was a waste of space and an impediment to my happiness. I became convinced that he disliked me for whatever reason. I was willing to let bygones be bygones, even though I wasn't sure what the thought or feeling represented––or whether it was genuine. When my father had the opportunity, he seldom gave up, breaking me down and leaving me hollow. Why couldn't he be Lucky's dad? Was I to blame for intransigence? I don't know. Parents are usually the source of the problem. I'm willing to accept responsibility.

My father's personality became more apparent to me as I grew older: false pride, complexes, and envy of others. He held some grudges. His parents, whom I don't recall ever meeting, were long dead, and his contact with them severed long before. Perhaps I wasn't the best listener to his stories about his childhood, parents, and grandparents. I would have liked to know what his parents might have been like and what kind of upbringing he had. Was he treated the same way he had treated Thomas or me? Given his tenacity, why was he so disappointed in me?

True, my mother had tried to explain my father's past: his unhappy childhood, loneliness, and unkindness in a low-income family with six siblings, and he had moved away to be rescued by a distant relative. My mother's words made little sense to me. I saw no logic and found no connection to his attitude towards me, possibly due to my reluctance or inability to grasp its complexities.

26

LONDON

I MADE WEEKLY ROUNDS in Charing Cross Road's bookshops on a bright autumn day. The brightness and warmth of the day surprised me because it felt exactly like summer. Summer days are primarily wet and cloudy, with few exceptions. The weather surprised me, as it was more suited for a stroll through Hyde Park or Regent's Park, taking in the wonderful ambience of either place. I felt compelled to remove my coat and the need to drink something. Perhaps coffee or tea or lemonade. No, I'd wait until noon.

An unshaven man with a pain-contorted expression, fifty or older, dressed in a grey-striped suit without a tie, began to address passers-by and soon approached me. What did he want? I had no desire for a cordial conversation with a stranger; I had my problems. Why hadn't my nonverbal communication conveyed that message? It was like being forced to choose between yes and no. My stroll had come to an abrupt halt. Sometimes the guilt overcame me after avoiding the beggars on the street. However, this time, it was possibly the type of beggar.

With a posh accent, the stranger struggled to deliver his speech: "I lo..., lost my wall..., my wallet that left, left me broke..." I got the gist of his message and began searching my pockets for loose change as the fellow continued to speak. He needed money for a cup of tea and a bun. His struggle to express himself had been embarrassingly painful for me to witness. I patiently listened to his desperate need.

I encountered beggars on the street of London and never understood why they frequently preferred me to indigenous peoples. Was it the absence of shame or the prospect of finding a sucker? I had no way of verifying the veracity of this man's claim. Through my heart's kindness and memory of mild stuttering during my childhood, I immediately felt an affinity with him. Was he a victim of unjust circumstances or the result of his actions? I offered the ostensibly poor guy three bobs; I couldn't afford more. I wished I could have afforded more because his need seemed more pressing than mine. I realised how fortunate I was; it was as if I needed others who were worse off than myself to feel worthy.

As I received the man's gratitude ("Thank... Thanks...sir!"), I nodded and resumed my way to the bookstores. Then suddenly, a smile appears on my lips: funny how some sequence of events can boost one's mood. Then tears began to well in my eyes, falling onto my cheeks. Maybe it was tears of sympathy for the poor guy or me.

I had written to my mother and Sandra about my act of kindness, which they praised as a divinely inspired moment. It was, of course, a Christian interpretation. I like to believe that some things are what they are, without meaning. This brief encounter reminded me that many people had it worse than I did. To be fair to my mother and Sandra, they could have been thinking about that lesson. The stranger with a stutter and a noble accent was black and was most likely born in Britain.

In Guyana, a few well-educated people had become homeless after having "going mad," as locals put it. One or two had studied and lived in the United Kingdom.

27

GEORGETOWN

ONCE, WHEN MY FATHER beat me, I cheekily told him: "You're wasting your time! It would be better to transform me into a sacrificial lamb by stabbing me in the heart, for I'm indeed *damaged goods.*"

His big bloodshot eyes grew more prominent as if possessed by a tormented bull in a ring, as if ready to deliver a lethal charge against the matador. My regular weight-lifting training had prepared me for a father-and-son battle because courage possessed me. I yanked the belt from his grip and threw it out a nearby window. Then, like a bolt of lightning, a punch landed squarely on my left side temple. The blow must have sent me to sleep.

I regained consciousness later while lying on the floor. My mother sat next to me on a chair. She was humming a hymn or praying while holding my hands. I can't recall anything.

When my dad became enraged, my mum usually got on her knees, put her head down, and prayed. And whenever I became the target, she often sought to come to my aid. As far as I can remember, her husband never raised a finger to harm her.

"Harry, I have bad news," my mother said. She paused, her tears welling up and falling.

"Your father wants you to leave the house by the time he returns, son. I'd tried to get him to change his mind. I told him it was an act of the devil to turn his back on his son. I said a prayer. I begged the Lord to lead me. What more can I do for you, Harry?"

I assured my mum it was all right and that she shouldn't be hard on herself. Trust the Lord, mum! I'll survive. The Lord was my only father, apart from Grandpa Adam, mum! I'll seek shelter at Grandpa's place.

My mother maintained her belief that "your father truly loves you, Harry." I heard a rebuttal uttered within: *Sure, he loves me, in a distorted way.*

Some say you always hurt the one you love. I always took it as an aphorism and nothing more.

I gathered a few of my belongings and hugged my mum, struggling to restrain my tears. I was undoubtedly in denial at some level. Tears streamed down my cheeks as I rode away with my bundle of belongings on my pushbike.

I spent a few days with Lucky's parents for a couple of days before heading to my grandpa's house.

Days later, I would continue to meet my mum, mostly at church, during her morning visits to the market, or on rare occasions for a stroll in the Botanical Gardens. She would then share cheerful tales from my early years: my first smile and attempts at walking, talking, running, and singing. She assured me that I would always be her one and only Harry.

My mum had avoided the unpleasant recollections, which suited me fine. I didn't want her or myself to be depressed. When we chose to be together, the amusing stuff served us well. I thought we both enjoyed it that way. Whenever I was low in spirit, I would attempt to be like my mum by quickly focusing on the positive.

I'd invested far too many negative thoughts I had no control over, which served me uncannily, perhaps as a boost to my battered self-esteem.

True, my loving and caring mum was there to console me. The power of love, like alcohol, appeared short-lived. In the face of extreme violence, such love was made powerless.

My mum must have suffered in silence, only sharing her emotional pain with the Lord Almighty. I never tried to talk to her about her suffering and pain. Some things are better left unsaid, to borrow a line from my father.

I told my mother about my desire to go to England. She appeared to recognise that I needed to leave my country and family. The time had come for me to seek a life of my own. My mum wanted me to have a happy and prosperous future.

I would say goodbye to my mother and father, Sandra, Faye and Thomas, my aunts and Grandpa Adam, friends, and Guyana less than a year later.

BOOK TWO

1

LONDON

I'D GO FOR A QUIET walk in the West End after picking up my dole at the Labour Exchange. It was my way of recalling images and events that I mentioned in letters to friends in my hometown. The West End's vibrancy, perhaps like that of the Big Apple, with an unending crowd milling about, going somewhere or nowhere, night and day. Entertainment venues, theatres, fashionable sections, nightclubs, discos, strip clubs, sex bookshops, restaurants, and cinemas. Why didn't I own a low-cost camera? In my letters, all of this and more were beyond comprehension.

Once, I was walking down the street with a friend when a man approached us handing out leaflets for a Soho club. The invitation invited the potential male customer to buy a drink for himself and a woman and engage in a cosy chat. The reality was that we could have paid for several drinks at an inflated price. The women received non-alcoholic beverages instead of whisky like ours. The place turned out to be a racketeering club: the two girls with whom my friend and I conversed wanted us to drink up and buy them more drinks. After the second round of drinks, we thought it best to exit the club before further trouble. Later we joked about inexperience carrying a price tag.

MY NEIGHBOURHOOD WAS Kingston, with a high percentage of white people, primarily British and Europeans. There could have been a few white American or Canadians, some wealthy, high-ranking Guyanese families, and the English pastor of our church as well as the Catholic Archbishop. One section of the neighbourhood was home to low-income families.

I was used to decent behaviour from English folks in my hometown. I had developed a romantic view of the English breed. In England, I became aware of different types of Englishness. The first couple of weeks, I took the Englishman at his word. But signs for job openings or rental rooms turned out to have a meaning of their own, or that unskilled labour required "previous experience." Such double-talk was beginning to confuse me.

I recall some instances where I logically understood what was happening. The situation was frequently not black or white but grey. It likely had a way of circumventing the law prohibiting racial prejudice or discrimination. In 1965, the "Race Relations Act" was passed. I'm thinking back to early 1962 when I first arrived in the United Kingdom.

When I arrived in England, much talk was about blacks and Asians coming to Britain. Enoch Powell's anti-immigration politics *Rivers of Blood* speech (1962) about London's streets or the entire English island.

All the talk about potential racial violence had me worried. I'd left a peaceful multicultural nation to start a new life in a country plagued by racial prejudice and racism. Perhaps I wasn't blind to the situation depicted in the newspapers in my hometown: that the UK was no bed of roses. I recall discussing newspaper accounts of the 1958 race riots in Notting Hill with schoolmates. Then there's my experience with the frequency of blatant denial in such matters, in the grey area. It wasn't always easy for people of colour to correctly point out racially discriminatory behaviour. In time, my romantic view of English fair play would fade over time, noticing its true colours: a display of pretexts, deceits, and denials. The Englishman appeared to have consoled himself by believing that the complainer was paranoid or had a chip on their shoulder, which sometimes may well have been the case.

It is simple to recognise and call out racial discrimination. Even if some accusations are false, dealing with persistent denial can be difficult. I had no chance against the Englishman's ethnic projections. Call my complaints paranoia.

My way of perceiving the world underwent a slightly disturbing change, though not alarming, not at the level of psychosis. My grandfather's nervous breakdown made me fearful of losing my mind in the foreseeable future. I read somewhere that insanity, at least schizophrenia, would probably occur in families, but not in every family or generation. When I think about it, healthy life depends on many factors: your genes, the environment, lifestyle, and happiness.

As a teenager, I attempted to replace antiquated ideas, thoughts, and beliefs with new ones. I enjoyed going to the cinema once or twice weekly. My favourite actors included Tony Curtis, Henry Fonda, Glen Ford, James Mason, John Wayne, and others. This habit persisted in England but clashed with the desire to read fiction and non-fiction and follow BBC television documentaries. And with realisation, I became interested in matters that appeal to the mind more than the body.

But it was a discord that made me uneasy. Later, I read an article or watched a BBC documentary about the human need to maintain our attitudes and beliefs to avoid disharmony.

I remained light-hearted in letters to friends and family. I didn't want to appear snobbish or send alarming signals about my health. My blues had settled on their own. I've read that mild depression can go away on its own. There was so much that the experts did not know about the human body, let alone the mind.

Nonetheless, I wouldn't delude myself into thinking I'm no longer worried about the anxiety attacks. In my letters to my sister Sandra, I would present vivid anecdotes with humour. I had written about my first visit to St. Paul's Cathedral in Wren. I wasn't interested in architecture as she was, although I could appreciate beautiful buildings, like Victorian buildings. One such structure was the West Indian Student Centre.

Heidi, a young German woman and a friend I had met in a Lutheran Church's social club, had invited me to a concert of Handel's Messiah. I did not enjoy the music and perhaps will, but I showed appreciation and gratitude by staying awake.

I remember Sandra and I used to, as children, visit the national library in downtown Georgetown on Main Street and South Road. She borrowed illustrated books of famous English and Italian architecture. I wrote to her about some English houses, most of which were in my neighbourhood from a layman's perspective. Two-storey, with tiny attics and windows that seemed to exist solely to let in light and draughts.

Such row houses, a series of tenement buildings not sufficiently separated to conceal the noise and commotion of the neighbour and more. No, such residences did not appeal to me since they were ancient and decrepit. In time, however, I realised the practicality of connecting attached homes. Guyana had space, whereas England did not.

Still, the inadequacy of some London homes bothered me as a tenant. They appeared to have been built in a hurry and without adequate inspection. The interior had shoddy construction and a lack of maintenance, with damped walls year-round. Window draughts made it impossible for a tenant like me in cold weather to be free of a sweater or cardigan and to suffer from cold hands and feet. The thought of winter made me wish there were three seasons in the annual cycle.

2

LONDON

IN SOCIAL LIFE IN THE West End, I ran into a fellow Guyanese from my neighbourhood, Kingston, in Georgetown, Guyana. Fred belonged to Sam's generation. We only knew each other as acquaintances. I was thrilled to meet someone from my community.

Fred Hamilton arrived in England a few years before I did. We met on my way to the British Council one early afternoon. He hadn't changed since the last time I saw him. The white of his eyes was still yellowish, just like my father's. He was tall and slim, with brown skin, freckles on his face, and ginger hair. Fred always appeared lean and wiry, with a flat stomach. Later, I learned about his discipline in maintaining a healthy physique, attending the gym regularly, and eating well.

Fred had a sense of humour as well. I first heard the phrase: "the Good, the Bad and the Ugly" from him, except for some things in life, perhaps nothing particularly new. The term exemplified Fred's habit of categorising others – viewing people as types.

Fred described himself as a realist regarding life. He could be cynical and express himself through dichotomies as good and evil, positive and negative, and so on. He gave the impression that he enjoyed reading about Western history, for he would make historical references to it, including World War II and the power Germany once had. His father was well-known in the neighbourhood for his admiration for Hitler. Fred, like his father, held the dictator in high esteem, impressed by

Hitler's brilliance. He denied that Hitler was a first-class fascist. Fred thought of him as a Messiah.

My knowledge of WWII was limited to my high school history books (written by Englishmen) and the opinions of Mr Murray, my history teacher with a walrus moustache. I'd crammed history, hoping to pass the exam by memorising dates, pinpointing significant events, and so on. But all this knowledge had faded from memory.

After that, I had fun hanging out with Fred in pubs or coffee bars in Leicester Square. I would tag along when he made trips to men's clothing stores, like Cecil Gee, Giorgio Armani, Ralph Lauren, or Harold's department store, in the evenings. Fred enjoyed the shop. He had the money because things there weren't cheap. Visiting shops, especially on Carnaby Street, was like a treat for me, admiring pretty birds with whom Fred chatted. I remember getting a little carried away.

Fred gave the impression of thoroughly knowing his way around the West End, flaunting his experience and knowledge. In one or more streets, he exchanged greetings in passing with some black brothers and whites chilling.

"While working in various jobs on Oxford Street, Tottenham Court Road, and High Street Kensington, I'd made connections with important people," Fred explained. "I used to work at Cook Travel Agency where I met some celebrities. And I know a few wealthy owners of nightclubs and well-known pubs."

What I liked best about Fred was how content he seemed with himself. In Guyana, he had attended a prestigious secondary school for boys in British Guyana, Queen's College. He came from a family with property and land. Fred's life had taken a wrong turn for some reason. A company where he worked had accused him of embezzlement but quickly withdrawn the accusation. Malicious gossip was that his wealthy father made a secret deal with the company through reimbursement and his son's resignation. Later, Fred and a friend opened a travel agency. They didn't take long to flee to an island in the

Caribbean, running with their customers' money. Several people had booked and paid for holidays. They were said to be hiding in Trinidad. I was in high school at the time.

Fred appeared to have cleaned up his act by going straight after a few years in England. Of course. That was my assumption. I had no reason to be sceptical or judgmental. Sam was aware of Fred's audacious criminal exploits in Guyana and judged Fred based on his previous deeds.

"You have to use your head in the Englishman's world," Fred said, gesturing as if to the rhythm of his speech. His adages often had a hint of advice in them. Fred wasn't as taken with educated people as I was. He bragged about being kicked out of Queen's College.

"Intelligence was one of the secrets to survival in any society. It existed in both educated and illiterate people," Fred said, adding, "I know people who hadn't worked a day and lived comfortably."

I did not fall for his roguish moral ethics, even though some of it was true. Fred had two brothers and three sisters. He was the youngest.

I was impressed that Fred regularly attended social gatherings like exhibitions in private art galleries, fashion shows and parties. He showed me such invitations. I saw evidence of a few famous black musicians in framed black and white photos on the walls in his flat in Primrose Hill, in Camden, NW London. I had the good fortune to accompany him three times. He wasn't a frequent drinker, usually brandy or gin and tonic. It was as though he wanted to keep a clear head and not be disadvantaged.

"Never trust or put your faith in anybody," he had once remarked.

Fred bore no similarity to the *bad apples* I befriended in Earl's Court. I had chosen to regard him as belonging to a higher league, perhaps conceding to Sam's view of him as "a rouge in disguise," a kind of scoundrel. Fred is doing well because he's good at gambling; he once told me: cards and roulette. Some folks I knew from his social background thought highly of themselves. No, not Fred.

Fred seemed different from Don and Leo in this sense. Both were much for a showy display of knowledge and sported cultivated British accents.

Don expressed himself with multisyllabic words. He spoke the way he wrote in a roundabout manner. At times his verbal expressions became incomprehensible, made so by legal terms and Latin words or phrases.

During Don and Leo's discussions, I wasn't always comfortable. Partly from an age difference, my low interest in current world affairs, and their allusion to things I had no idea of or was far too above my head.

Usually, I would shy away from such topics, which the two men mainly discussed among themselves. Don was a solicitor at a law firm in Peckham, and Leo was an economist who worked for British Railways. Leo suffered from a stomach ulcer, usually after dinner. Don dated English and Caribbean women, while Leo dated continental women, mainly German and French. He spoke both languages.

Fred and I went to a cafe near the Piccadilly Circus, where we met some of the regular West Indians. Fred knew men who didn't have steady jobs but with a grand dream of living a life of luxury. They seemed to spend much time in the cafe talking, boasting, and laughing about events that might have taken place in their lives in the past. The heroes they worshipped were either deported or received lengthy sentences. They talked about race-horse gambling, integration issues, and the "enemy" (Enoch Powell's supporters).

I found the cafe an exciting place. It was a sort of "West Indian haven" (Fred's description) for Caribbean men. Their lives might have been marginalised in their home countries, and their status remained the same in "the mother country."

Years later, I considered myself a marginal figure in the UK.

A SCENE I REMEMBERED where the weather was changeable, and a clique of Caribbean men sit with cups of tea or bottles of beer in a dingy cafe in a basement in Ladbroke Grove. The men reminisced, exploring "the black man's burden", which could be bigotry, racism, xenophobia, or all three) in England, the mother country.

Fred took me there; he says he likes to drop by sometimes to hear about life on the side of the black existence spectrum.

Fred: "Hello, guys! I brought a friend along. He came up not too long ago from GT (Georgetown)."

In harmony, two of them say, as if rehearsed, "New Boy!" Some smiled, others seemed to stare in wonder, or their minds may have been on the discussion.

Fred: "*Continue the talk, me listening, man!*"

Eddie: "*Like ... like me was sayin', some t'ings was bet-ta bay-fore in dis cunt-tree.*"

Billy, who sat next to him, seemed to agree; his head was bobbing away. "Dat's *for sure.*"

Danny: "*English folks: dem was easier to know.*"

Jimmy: "*Der was work, and social life was friend-lee-like.*"

Keith: "*Yes, ordinary folks was friendlee-er. A black man was a novel-tee den.*"

Billy rejoices: "*But we wasn't plen-tee in dem days.*"

Danny: "*Bee-fore t'ings start to get worse.*"

Eddie: "*Ordinary Eng-a-lish man, gettin' frighten, gettin' jealous 'bout us datin' white woo-men.*"

Jimmy: "*Po-lit-tee-cal propa-ganda full-up dey heads with lies. Dem start to fear us.*"

Keith: "*Accus-ing us for takin' deer jobs too. What silly shit!*"

Eddie: "*Plain jeal-ous-ness, that's all. Dem had nothin' to be frighten' 'bout.*"

Joey: "*Dem had somethin' all right. Fear, sometimes, come from a good cause.*"

Billy: "*W'at yo' mean?*"

Joey: "*Boatloads with pee-pull from back home and India! Dat's what I mean to say.*"

Billy's head bobs away: "*Good point! Too many like we was comming' here. Sure, mess up dee scene! Dem bring their rude ways too!*"

Danny: "*Boatloads spoil tings for us. British people turn angry?*"

Joe: "*Yo better believe it. We're no longer welcome.*"

Keith: "*It is confusin'. Dem kind of work we do, de English skin-up dear faces at! Dem a fretful pee-pill, if yo' axe me.*"

Eddie: "*That's why I say it is plain jealous-ness, man! No logic! Just hu-man bad-feelin'.*"

Keith: "*Still confusin', man. Didn't de Transport bosses went and fetched pee-pull from Barbados to run the buses and trains? We for-gettin' dat.*"

Fred interjected, with a touch of Creole, as if he didn't wish to set himself above the men: "*All politics! The blaming game, scapegoat tactics. Dis once great cunt-tree never was Earthly paradise. Some of its cities built from 'sweat of slavery'. Also, London got a pounding from Hitler flying machines. Some of the mess, black folks help to clean up. They forget our bit in the war effort!*"

Eddie: "*We sure did the clean-up. But dat was a long time ago. Pee-pull have short me-mo-ree, and much of dem wasn't even born*".

I mused for a while about their complaints and nostalgia. The fruit trees planted in the past by various black labour have turned sour. Should I follow their gloomy message and throw my dreams of a better life to the wind? Was I treading the soil of a wasteland, judging from the accounts of a few disgruntled voices? I reflected on what would it be like to follow Fred's path, a supposed villain? It wasn't a sure thing for me, a coward.

In a corner chair, away from the clique of men, sat Dexter, who suffered from mental ill-health. Fred later informed me. Each day Dexter received a free meal. Dexter's monologue, which had received no attention, added to the men's discourse. The clique of men appeared neglectful of his utterances.

I heard him say: "... *the bullshit the colonial blacks suffered at the hands of Brits who look down on us with scorn and hate on their faces, and we look down on ourselves. Mixed children have an attitude towards us, elderly immigrants. Instead of pride for us who fought in the war, they show hate and shame. White fathers...upset about their daughters' mingling with my son. What 'bout my three daughters and the pumping they get from white blokes? One-sided affair. The world's what it is, a shit hole of a place!*"

The bitterness dwells in the mind of a troubled soul, residing with me for a good while that day.

IT WAS LUNCHTIME AND a revisit to the Grove. Fred took me to Sony's Cafe, where I ate black-eyed peas, rice, and stew biff before following the crowd with carrot juice.

"Damn good cook," I exclaimed, picking my teeth.

Afterwards, we headed for "the Court" (Earl's Court), where a friend of Fred's owned a business. The purchase of marijuana (or ganja) and smoking it in this fellah's tiny tenement room in a basement; a bit messy and smelly - a sort of speakeasy for illegal selling of alcohol: Demerara Rum and other Caribbean brands. "Stormy Monday Blues" flowed from a pair of tiny loudspeakers at a moderate tone and added to the here-and-now ambience.

3

LONDON

UNEMPLOYMENT REMAINED a feature of my and many young people's lives. I was astonished because there weren't young people at the Labour Exchange when I went. The youngsters probably were somewhere else or appeared on different days.

The Macmillan government expressed concern about the number of young people out of work. I stated that it was doing everything possible to reverse the trend. The Labour Party, the leading opposition party, said that given a chance to govern, it would solve the problem. The media criticised the government, and the trade union movement targeted some employers that hired "cheap immigrant labour." The media have also criticised unemployed young people.

Much of this information came from reading the Evening News and watching BBC television discussions.

I had my opinions on the unemployment issue. The media blamed the youth. I assumed the journalists belonged to an older generation. Still, I believed that English youths were having difficulty finding work. It surprised me that the media did not discuss foreigners' difficulty finding employment. The notion that foreigners found jobs because of their willingness to accept low wages was probably correct. Still, it was not something I was willing to do.

Sam called to check on how things were going. I was embarrassed that I was still unemployed to be still out and suspected that my father wanted him to spy on me. My mother once wrote that they had communicated with one another. My father always praised Sam for being "a gentleman with an ambition to go far in life." I had no contact with my dad directly, only through my mum's letters.

We've spoken on the phone a few times, and it's been nothing more than courtesy. I served up the positives: my consistent effort to find work and that I had a job interview but stressed that it was not clerical. I changed the subject by mentioning frequent library visits and meeting some new friends at the Student Centre and in the West End. Saying the West End had not been a good idea. It prompted Sam to warn me about *worthless types from Guyana and the Caribbean who frequented the West End.*

My father's admiration for Sam was clear to me. He reminded me of some of the ambitious people I knew in Guyana. He wasn't the only one who aspired to be a lawyer. I met several people on the same path at the Student Centre. There was a colony of lawyers in Guyana. Many of them were of African descent. Few became successful barristers, but some went on to careers in Guyana as administrators, politicians, magistrates, and lawyers. JOF Haynes, Fred Wills, Rex McKay, and other distinguished barristers––criminal and civil bars––impressed me with their brilliance and articulation.

Sam was starting to irritate me on the phone. But I kept my calm. I may have been too open about my desires in life, my uncertainty about which path to take: the ups and downs of life's journey.

I also mentioned Guyanese Fred by mistake. Sam regarded him as "a shady figure." He was certain Fred would mislead me. I remained silent.

"Take my word for it," Sam said, sounding eerily like my father. I resolved to call him less frequently. He had shifted from being supportive to being judgmental.

4

LONDON

THE IDEA OF RETURNING to Guyana was behind me.

"You would be a chicken to return to the safe wings of mother-hen," Fred said over the phone.

"It would appear so," I said, standing in the Student Centre's phone booth, killing time before dinner began.

"Live life without breaking a sweat," he said. "Things happen in our lives for a reason. Remember, the Labour Exchange was founded on the notion that no one should go hungry or homeless."

Strangely, Sam's remark that *the Labour Exchange wasn't thy brother's keeper* popped into my head as if to counter Fred's. Both observations appeared plausible.

Fred was probably correct when he said that I shouldn't take life too seriously because life has a way of changing for the better of its volition.

"Didn't you see Georgetown riots on BBC?" he said.

"Yeah, I watched some of it here at the Student Centre," I said, alluding that they were now serving dinner. "I recognised a few people interviewed by a BBC reporter, each of whom expressed a desire to immigrate to the UK. I have good reason to be grateful, Fred." I laughed at the thought of wanting to go back to Guyana.

Fred laughed, and the conversation came to an end.

I arrived in England on Feb 14th, 1962. And on Feb 12th, 1962, a union strike against the ruling party (PPP) and its austerity budget began. Sandra wrote to me that my father was a harsh critic of the protesters. He was concerned about the breakdown of law and order. The vandalising of property and the stealing of merchandise occurred. Sandra also mentioned that red-skinned Frank, from the neighbourhood, was killed, allegedly by a police rifle stray bullet during the rioting and looting. He hadn't been a close friend, but a friend, nonetheless.

5
LONDON

I WAS ON MY WAY TO the Labour Exchange, as is compulsory. *Will there be a change of luck?* I was perplexed. I had missed breakfast due to my excessive snoozing. Since I was a teenager, I've struggled with punctuality. My stomach was screaming hunger cries. I needed a sandwich or fruit on my way out, but I was afraid of missing the bus and the Tube.

The Labour Exchange officials are entitled to be candid about your late coming, and rightly so. I was determined to arrive on time. I passed a confectionary shop, a bakery, and a cafeteria. Which one would be practical? In such stressful situations, I tended to make the wrong decision. It would be nice to have a doughnut or a small cake. But common sense urged me to settle for a bakery bun because my love for wheat, salt, and sugar was still strong. There was no line, which was fortunate for me. Although we have a robust memory of misfortune, there is such a thing as good luck.

I arrived at the Labour Exchange on time. The official showed a smiling face. Was it a good omen or a bad omen? Because I had to wait, I sat two seats from the nearest person. I opened the small brown paper bag, broke a piece of the bun, and placed it discreetly in my mouth, closing it and chewing––the way my father always insisted. I looked around. There aren't many visitors here.

Another piece of bun found its way into my mouth. A woman and child now had their eyes on me, making me self-conscious. I would like to know if I might need to improve in etiquette. I dismissed the thought and felt justified in my behaviour.

In Georgetown and London, people of all kinds were always watching me for whatever reason. I pondered if it was a mindless or compulsive activity. The desire was probably universal, or if it wasn't my eating, it could have been my presence for simply being there. In the case of children, I assumed their staring was motivated by curiosity. As with adults, there was probably the habit of critical or absentminded observation when there was nothing else to do. After all, we are social animals. People need people to hate or love. Life can be exceedingly dull at times.

As I heard my name from a loudspeaker instructing me to enter booth 4, my mouth opened to receive the third and final piece of the bun. I jumped and tossed a squeezed paper bag into a waste basket.

"Good morning, Mr Holmes," said the short, skinny, and pale official after clearing his throat. The tendency to clean one's throat: It was difficult to determine whether the behaviour was driven by a genuine need. His demeanour was gentle and soft, and his face appeared younger for someone with greying hair on the sides. His hands appeared larger for his small stature.

I greeted him good morning, and he motioned for me to sit. As his right hand traced the contour of a button at the breast of his brown jacket, he cleared his throat. I decided to calm my nerves. I wanted to know if I could control my irrational beliefs in a situation like this.

"You've been without work for some time," he said, leafing through my file.

"That's correct." I had in mind to expand but decided there was no need to justify my unfortunate situation.

"I see you've been made redundant from your first and only job," he said, looking at me.

"Yes. That's correct. I had a bit of bad luck."

"You have a lot of bad luck securing work, Mr Holmes. Wouldn't you say?" he said, clearing his throat.

"That's true. I arrived in England at the wrong time and didn't know it would be an insurmountable obstacle." There I was, appealing for compassion and understanding.

"We mustn't lose hope, Mr Holmes." He said in an impersonal manner. He handed me a notice of vacancy.

"It's a vacancy at an industrial plant. This time, a spot of luck may be on your side, Mr Holmes."

I expressed my gratitude to the official for his well-wishes. As we parted, he nodded and cleared his throat.

I took the official's comments seriously, but they wounded my dignity. I may ultimately resort to verbal abuse against anyone who offends me most slightly.

I struggled to understand my need to throw tantrums, piling insult after insult, until I exploded. I found a book describing the problem while browsing through books at Foyles. It was about storing hurt feelings and insults like toxic waste, then letting it fall apart in a shocking display of emotional debris, usually over minor offences. You are embarrassed and ready to ask for forgiveness. I'm not in the habit of diagnosing myself or others. It could be beneficial when treating persons with extreme personality disorders who need mental health care.

The job vacancy was for a sweeper. I would have to ring and make an appointment for a job interview. I mumbled on my way to the Tube but decided not to get grumpy or gloomy, as if mood changes were up to the individual--I read somewhere.

6

LONDON

IF THE INTERVIEW FAILS, I might consider joining the British Army. Still, I couldn't imagine fighting British battles, let alone my own. But the delusion persisted.

The Army of Her Majesty. So, what's the harm? Blimey! Let's face it: my identity is--well, I'm not sure. Perhaps puzzling, but not a split personality; instead, a guy born and reared in a British colony to serve the Queen.

For some time, the fantasy has been swirling in my head. Off and on. The benefits included developing a healthy physique, learning a trade, travelling to different countries, and impressing "birds." Joining the navy would be safer at arm's length distance from rifle fire! All of this, however, was a romantic fantasy.

The presumption was that the negatives represented an assortment of unattractive characteristics of army life. In all seasons, I wake up (movie-style) to the sound of a bugle at dawn. I see myself in trunks and T-shirts, jogging in temperatures below zero degrees Celsius, or jumping or overpowering obstacles. Maybe I'd have to take cold baths, do long drills, and have sergeants yell at me (which would probably remind me of my distraught father) until I fainted or went berserk. Like myself, I'm sure those young men had gone through a lot. Where there is a will, there is a way, my father would say.

No. No thanks! I may have a streak of masochism, but not to the extent that I could withstand everything that sadistic sergeants were likely to throw at Private Harry Holmes. No, sir! Joining the Army would also put me in awkward situations with authoritative figures.

I'd escaped from the ordeal by pure chance. The truth is that I did not go to the Army recruiting office; I took a written test for the Air Force that didn't go well, owing to nerves, of course. So, my results only qualified me to join the Army. Given the status, I had thought of the Air Force at the spur of the moment.

To be part of the Army, I had two weeks to decide.

Two years was enough to acquire a trade, get out in one piece, and be a valuable reference when looking for work.

I told my flatmates in Chelsea and some friends at the Student Centre. The general advice or response was pessimistic.

"Don't throw your future away," Don and Leo said almost simultaneously. "Better things to do than becoming a soldier, going to foreign countries searching for enemies." They both laughed.

I, too, scoffed at the notion of surrendering my life in the manner of a Jesus figure.

"Study instead, at evening classes, then go back to Guyana and help develop the country," Percival said, a friend at the Student Centre. He was a Jamaican and a student of engineering.

Studying or returning to Guyana was never on my agenda, though I avoided mentioning it, possibly out of shame. I wasn't as patriotic as he, but I could appreciate his love for his country.

I was never devoted to any country, although I did miss the Guyana of my boyhood. It took me two trips to grasp that *my* Guyana was no longer the same. Maybe we'd both changed.

I once wished to become an American citizen, but the wish did not last.

Instead of love for nations, there would be love and affection for friends and family in the United States, the United Kingdom, Guyana,

Sweden, and the United States. The Italian region of Tuscany, Florence, London, New York, Paris, Stockholm, and Venice.

7

LONDON

THE DAY OF THE JOB interview arrived. I had to be at the factory office for nine. I left home at 07.45. There was severe rainfall and flooding on certain roadways and lengthy bus lines. My shoes, socks, and trousers got wet from splashing water from a speeding vehicle during a short distance to the Tube station. An umbrella could have shielded me from the splash. I tried not to interpret the weather and incident as bad omens. Interestingly, I wasn't nervous, even though the dreadful London Transport interview made me vary in job interviews. Today's meeting was not about a dream job but rather about getting my weary backside off the unemployment bench.

I decided against wearing my Sunday best suit and tie. I wanted to look the part, unskilled, which I was. Overdressing might be enough to dissuade the interviewer.

The interview went much better than anticipated. Ms Molly O'Connor was an Irish woman who conducted the interview. She was a bit of a chatterbox, but she was friendly as if we knew each other, and I believed her manner was genuine, though I couldn't be sure.

There weren't many questions about prior experiences or anything like that. I decided not to overdo things by speaking out of turn or showing off my general knowledge or wit. I laid out my cards about my dire situation since arriving in England. I had the impression she liked me (whatever that meant), which helped calm my nerves.

Finally, Ms O'Connor informed me that I would receive an answer by mail. My heart skipped a beat, hoping for an answer right there and then. Such is life, I reasoned, reminding myself to remain optimistic.

Did it make a difference back then to think positively? Although many Christians believe that positive thinking makes a difference, I'm not convinced. Christians were an optimistic bunch, though they could also be pessimistic. Of course, they hoped to go to heaven after leaving behind the trials and tribulations of human existence. To my mother, "Life on Earth" was a trial run for life after death.

8

LONDON

I WAS ON MY WAY TO a party at Fred's place one windy late Friday evening in West Hampstead. When I arrived, the pad was packed. The party was in full swing, with several mixed couples and a few feminine-looking men, black and white, all attendees engaged in small talk, amusement, and laughter. From a distance, the host greeted me; he conversed with an older white bloke, business-like. They appeared to be going through some notebooks.

In the background, Classic jazz came from small-sized speakers—a decent three-room pad. I had anticipated a large display of expensive-looking furniture and items. It was, however, modestly decorated, cosy and tidy. Framed black-and-white photographs adorned the walls: Miles Davis, Thelonious Monk, Charlie Parker, Ben Webster, Dinah Washington, Sarah Vaughan, and a few landscapes. There were drinks, nuts, and chips available. That was all there was to eat.

I expected food as with home parties hosted by West Indians. Someone yelled: "start the smokes." I missed the point. A lighted cigarette soon passed from person to person, and I followed suit.

"Lanky John," someone called out. He nodded his head, hair in dreadlocks, eyes closed as he smoked and danced solo to a short jazzy piece. They were all strangers to me, except for Fred.

I've always had a thing for pretty faces. I regarded an attractive thirty-something woman. She wasn't alone, accompanied by a bearded black guy twice my body size and much older than her. He wore a white suit with a pink bow tie. He appeared to be chatty, whereas she seemed quiet.

A few men wore black leather jackets as though they were members of a gang or lodge. They appeared like shady figures or even hustlers. They sported sunglasses.

I ought to get myself a leather jacket, but I prefer a brown one. It would have to wait.

The wine or smoking was getting to me. I laughed. A blissful feeling as if I were floating on clouds and a slightly blurred sensation. The woman I fancied became a double figure. She shouted, "For a change, play some Beatles!" Her speech was squeaky, which contrasted with her beauty. I already spotted this flaw, and probably more in store for me. I smiled at the thought, an imperfection, and so often the case.

Neurotic women tended to draw me: a jumble of this and that, belligerent and teetering on some mental condition. I could love such a woman, but only for some months if it took that long before the yearning dissipated. In Guyana, I met some gorgeous, charming, and seductive girlfriends. But it never progressed beyond platonic love.

All this is probably a projection. We--flawed souls--fared poorly in romantic relationships, most likely because we sought perfection rather than someone with demons compatible with ours.

"Cool it with the damn jazz, please!" came from a woman's voice. "Manfred Mann, please!" then a round of laughter followed.

Pointing to the woman with a squeaky voice, I asked Fred about her status.

"The lady is not a one-man type," he said straight-faced.

I was encouraged by his remark and will try to forget her voice. Perhaps alcohol, smoking, or a combination of both might've impaired my hearing. I wouldn't dare to make a move on the lady in question since I wasn't myself. I'll save the adventure for another day.

9

LONDON

I WAS PLEASED WITH how things were going; I found a place on my own. I may be on the road to self-reliance. All of this would eventually contribute to my happiness. My self-confidence, however, remained a problem, and I was still desperate for advice to have more confidence in others.

I trusted my mother and my sister Sandra. Thomas and Faye's harmonious relationship with our father was most likely due to doing with the distance between them and me. I'm distrustful of anyone with close ties with me and anyone with whom I had bad vibes. That, I will admit, remains one of my quirks.

My efforts to join the British workforce continued. Many rejection letters, so there was no need to impress officials at the Labour Exchange. The file system was Fred's idea.

Despite numerous written rejections, I was no longer disappointed or disheartened. I attributed the pleasant sensation to Fred. I kept a low profile during interviews where politeness was the rule. I recall a restaurant where the manager offered me a free lunch as if his refusal to accommodate my request for a dishwasher hadn't been personal. Could I have accused him of deception? I recalled saying no, thank you, and smiling.

Such faux courtesy was prevalent in London as if it were part of the city's protocol. Was it a fragment of my imagination, as some English people would probably claim? Nevertheless, experience has taught me. I was learning to ape the manner of some English people. I let rid of my simplicity and shed the feathers of my innocence. In a way and the attitude of some English people, London had become my Mecca. It took years to understand the change taking place in my life at the time.

I had lost faith in religion or religious people, but the two should be distinct. Was I turning into a misanthropist or an atheist? Or was I an agnostic, playing it safe? At the time, I didn't see it in that light. I still "believe in something larger than life," which could have been a humanistic perspective on life, which wasn't all that different from Christianity, save for Heaven and Hell. Perhaps an agnostic book I came across had an impact on me.

Aside from alleviating mild depression, I noticed that my anxiety attacks became less frequent. I'm not sure why that was the case. I was trying not to worry too much, to have faith in the future, and to remember that patience was essential.

A thank you to my GP for being supportive. A thank you to Don and Leo for allowing me to stay with them at a time of great need. Although Fred and I were different, I benefited somewhat from his friendship.

There was now an insatiable desire for my chosen knowledge and self-development through excessive reading. Different from the traditional approach found within the academic learning walls: selected, categorised, along the lines of established patterns and scientific. Instead, finding an unskilled job that did not require certified knowledge suited me perfectly. Later, I developed a positive attitude by understanding the value of academic learning, thought, discipline and thinking.

My library visits persisted. I began by reading several books by Bertram Russell. I learned a lot from his writings, whether I got them right or not. His clear and straightforward writing style, his gift of persuasion, and his opinions, thoughts, and beliefs motivated me. I wanted to express myself clearly in writing and speech, particularly in correspondence with officials. Later, I purchased paperback books on anthropology, psychology, philosophy, and sociology. My reading list also included history (African, American, British, and West Indian) and literature (books by English authors and black and white American novelists).

In that order, reading became as important to me as listening to my favourite music (jazz, r&b, and soul), going on dates, or meeting up with friends.

AUTUMN BROUGHT A LOT of drizzles, storms, and falling leaves. When the cold season returned, my fingers and feet suffered. The arrival of gale-force winds prepared me for what was to come when severe winters arrived. What I imagined were long, cold, and snowy days. My walking speed had increased, and my hands would continue to seek refuge in my light overcoat or jacket pockets. If my feet didn't suffer too much from the cold, I'd have to think about investing in a proper winter coat and woolly socks. Oh, the imagination! How neatly and simply it organises one's wishes! To imagine it became a pleasant pastime.

10

LONDON

ANOTHER SOURCE OF DISCONTENT appeared in my life, which wasn't new but seemed to be a recurring annoyance. It stemmed from my dating. Maggie, with a lovely face, was at Fred's party. Fred followed through with his promise to introduce me. He had taken me to Maggie's favourite pub. He had told her I wanted to meet her and everything else, which elicited her guffaw and distorted her pretty face. And the way she looked at me from head to toe reminded me of how some girls greeted my request for a dance at parties or dances in Guyana. I offered Fred and Maggie a drink after we exchanged handshakes. Maggie accepted. Fred needed to run some errands.

I immediately noticed an increased heart rate, sweating, dry throat, and slight dizziness. The line moved slowly, and the need for air grew urgent. I went outside to get some fresh air. My posture was stiff. I did some deep breathing exercises while concentrating (a distracting technique), counting backwards from a thousand. When I returned, the line had shrunk, and I was a little shaken, but the worst was over.

Maggie received a glass of Babycham and a medium-sized beer for me.

"Cheers!" I said. Our glasses touched.

"Cheers!" Maggie said, smiling.

"Do you come here a lot?" I said, taking a sip and smiling earnestly.

"Sometimes." Her voice wasn't as squeaky as the night at Fred's party.

"Where in the West Indies are you from?" she asked, sipping her Babycham.

"What other places do you enjoy going to? I said.

"Wow, that's a tough one!" Maggie burst out laughing as she said this. "Well, you were at Fred's party. I recognised your face."

I nodded. My face was still bright.

"Things like parties, movies, and getting together with friends," Maggie said, reaching for a pack of cigarettes and a lighter from her purple shoulder bag. She offered me a cigarette while lighting one between her black lipstick lips. I politely declined.

I drank some beer. My anxiety had vanished.

Following a brief pause, I presented a condensed version of myself: essentials and inessentials.

Maggie nodded away, her head slightly tilted to the ceiling, her mouth inhaling and exhaling smoke. Her gaze shifted once or twice during the conversation.

She didn't have any questions after I finished, so I asked if she was a student.

"A student? Do I look like one? she giggled before inhaling and exhaling.

"It was just a thought."

"I've had enough of schools; learn from everyday life, from people I know and don't know," Maggie said.

"I'm a little fed-up with studying," I found myself saying.

"Fred says street life is the finest college!" she said.

"I understand his point, but things are rarely good or bad."

Maggie chuckled as she observed other pub guests. She drank the last of her Babycham and took the last puff from her cigarette.

I wasn't sure why she laughed, but I decided not to ask. Maggie smiled and acted like another person. She seemed a different person from the impression I got from Fred.

"What's your name again, and what do you think of London?" she said.

I expressed a couple of mixed emotions.

"So, you aren't having a good time! Disappointed, are you?" Her eyebrows furrowed

"Yes, you could say that," I said and finished my beer.

"I know a few West Indians who come to England with plans. Some performed well and returned home. Fred knew several people who committed suicide or got admitted to psychiatric hospitals. For many newcomers, life in London can be hell. Similar tragedies occur among young English people from counties," Maggie said.

"Wretched," I said.

There was a pause. Both Maggie and I looked at other customers. I looked forward to a lovely date with Maggie, but my serious-mindedness got the better of me.

"Can you tell me about your favourite music and movies?" I said, interrupting the conversation.

"That's funny you asked that. I can't live without music," Maggie said, her face brightened. "To be honest, not many blues or jazz. Fred is a jazz fanatic!"

"Keep going. I'm listening." Finally, I felt at ease, as if I were in control and on my way to an enjoyable first date.

"British pop music on radio and TV," she said as she lit another cigarette, taking a deep breath and exhaling. "And before I forget, Jamaican Ska music. When it comes to movies, many English films: Maybe more American movies, like Gone with the Wind, Casablanca, and Singing in the Rain. There are too many to name." She laughed, breathed in, and breathed out smoke. She seemed to be in her element.

"Comedy and some scary parts. I go to the movies often." Did you get a hint? I began to feel hot. There were a lot of people in the pub.

"It's getting crowded here."

"It could get worse," she said.

"Why don't we go somewhere friendlier for conversation?"

"Why not! What do you have in mind?" Maggie said.

"Nothing," I said, "I wished I lived nearby."

"No one I know can afford to live in the neighbourhood," she said. "I live in Willesden Green," Maggie said.

She and I decided to stroll around Piccadilly Circus in the evening. I then acquired her phone number and vowed to call her.

I called Maggie about a week later. It took her a bit to recall who I was. After hearing her chuckle, I proposed a movie date or a night at the disco.

"Both places I only go with my husband," she said.

"I see," I said. *So, Maggie is married*, I mused. "Maybe it was him at Fred's party", I asked her.

"Who was that?" Maggie said. "He wasn't there!"

"Oh! I got it wrong!" I described the fellow to her.

"Oh, him!" Maggie said after a little pause. No, no! "An acquaintance!"

But it didn't matter, I thought. Maggie had a husband, or was lying, or whatever. I tried to appear calm. I alluded to the weather and ended with, "Well, Maggie, see you around!"

She said, in a singsong tone, "Thanks for calling! Bye!"

The telephone chat left me in a pissed mood. What was that? For starters, why did she give me her number? Was she a teaser or not right in her mind? Questions, questions, questions! Two genders with different mindsets.

Later I informed Fred about Maggie's change of heart or whatever it was.

He said: "She had a husband, but he's a seaman on a Canadian ship, absent three months or longer at a time."

Fred said, "Man, you mean yo' swallow that pill," and sounded like a naughty kid in his creole style. Even mature men can, at times, be childlike.

I asked, "Why did she say this as though to mislead me?" Could I have handled the situation cleverly, keeping calm while insisting on a date? I wasn't that type of person.

Fred shook his head. "It sounded as if Maggie was testing you, man. I know her. At times, she can be like that. It's her way of knowing if you have what it takes!"

"Yo' know, London isn't Georgetown! In London, things are different. I should have warned you. But there's nothing better than experience!" Fred laughed. He was right: nothing like experience.

I found myself laughing too. "No need for me to get uptight. I'd messed up," I said as if thinking aloud, adding, "But Maggie sounded genuine! I thought I read her correctly."

Fred said: "Man, how long yo' know women? Maggie is the sort of woman that would stare yo' in the eye and lie."

"Ha-ha," I said, in bare-face-like, "like some girls back home."

"That's Maggie's way of determining whether yo' are a man or boy! By the look of it, she got the answer. If Maggie likes yo', she'll give yo' a pass, meaning: Yo' still have a chance!" Fred smiled.

"She's okay but shrewd! She can teach you a thing or two."

"Okay, I get your meaning!"

That's what I liked about hanging out with streetwise folks and older folks. I confessed to Fred that I wanted to mature as quickly as possible by learning stuff we didn't learn in school. Fred said he understood this and, as a newcomer, it was a natural desire to talk about Guyana and my ambitions and problems finding a job. I was astonished when he said that.

So, Maggie had gossiped about me. I laughed. To have heard about it, I couldn't help thinking now that I probably formed a wrong impression, like a schoolboy. Of course, there was no reasonable basis other than my suspicious mind.

"And one thing more. Some women can be the mothering type to young men. Maggie isn't one. So be watchful of such a desire, especially for some men with strong ties to their mothers. Learn to be cool and rational during the first encounter. The first impressions can be lasting. Listen more, talk less, particularly about yourself; learn more about the woman's character and personality. London isn't Georgetown, where you must coax and apply patience. You'll soon learn to forget the Guyanese "boy-and-girl-friend thing." Think of a woman's likes and dislikes. Don't always like the things she likes. It's all about understanding and grasping the situation. Dig?"

It would be intricate; I remember thinking. That man-and-woman relationship wasn't uncomplicated. Preparing for a school exam seemed more manageable. I had to learn a new approach to women. In Guyana, I read *The Second Sex* by Simone de Beauvoir and acquired some knowledge, but there is nothing better than first-hand knowledge. I will see what the future holds.

Maggie was 36, with a pretty face and an engaging smile, though her face seemed less attractive when she laughed. My interest was lascivious: thick thighs, legs, calves, a rolling backside, and a graceful gait.

I knew I was more attracted to her body than her personality or character. I can see my curiosity about her nature developing. Had I been taught to objectify the opposite sex, or was it my hormone? What was so indecent about admiring a woman's body? Does this imply that I solely see her as a sexual object? A woman's interest in a man may begin with his personality, with exceptions.

I felt embarrassed. I always wanted to appear calm and relaxed in the manner of Fred and his friends, especially the ones in leather jackets, though minus my suspicions of their involvement in illegal dealings or some other trading. Would I get another go at Maggie?

Weeks later, I happened to bump into her in another pub. I went to her and insisted on getting her a drink. This time, it was a gin and tonic and a cream label for me. I then continued to unfold my new approach (after rehearsing it a few times, an old practice of mine during my high school years). I then adopted a macho manner and explained my romantic desires. My performance felt impeccable. But Maggie did not fall for my theatrics. Fred might've been talking through his hat, though he did get it correctly about the effect of the first impression. There wasn't a second chance.

I consoled myself that Maggie was too sophisticated for me, which was a lame excuse.

In time, I may disparage her in thought to salvage a wounded ego: probably the whole town was sleeping, or had slept, with her and that she wasn't my type. I even had her down to be a pimp's lady, which carried things too far.

My father used to say I was born with a vindictive streak. Who was he to judge me? I was a copy of him. My mother was right. I was like him, though I always loathed the insight. It's odd how some things turn out to be in your life: being like a parent you dislike.

My failure with Maggie conveyed the meaning of an old saying: Never judge books by their covers. The truth was that I continued to judge books by their covers.

11

LONDON

FRED HEARD FROM ME that it didn't go down well with Maggie and that I may have overdone it. He advised me not to overthink the disappointment that comes with human connections. "You're still young!" Maggie is considerably older and wiser. Some people make the same mistake repeatedly. Forget about Maggie.

"I had grown used to not consistently having my way and had learned to wipe away the failures. For some men, it comes with age. Others remain crybabies and lose themselves to self-destruction," Fred once said.

I remembered smiling at his casual approach of avoiding grief and keeping emotional discomfort at arm's length. Perhaps this was a hardened attitude. He reminded me of tough guys in American noir films from the 1940s I saw in the 1950s. Actors like Humphrey Bogart, George Raft, James Cagney, Edward G. Robinson, and others. Was it down to experience with Fred, or did he seek solitude and get high on marijuana? I did not doubt that he was straight with me. I had observed he appeared to be unperturbed. How were some people quickly troubled while others didn't care a damn? Incredible. I was so easily hurt.

Sometimes I wondered about the character, the personality, and the lives of others. How did Fred become Fred (and how did I become who I am)? Did he have Samuel Holmes for a father or Thelma Holmes for a mother or vice versa? To what extent were we the product of our parents or guardians? Some say our environment played a part in our character; something happened long before birth. Others remain steadfast in the belief that we can't escape the influence of our genes. Hmm! I considered life a mystery. Considering God as the Creator of life solves the riddle, I sometimes wonder about the Christian faith. Christians say that reason cannot understand religion only through faith. I was thinking of all the evil that existed and still exists.

On Wednesday evening, Fred had invited me to tag along at the Astoria. He donned a grey suit without a tie, a blue satin scarf stylishly wrapped around his neck and tucked into the collar of a light blue shirt. On his feet was a pair of black and white Bailey shoes.

I wore a pair of tightly fitted brown trousers, slightly above the ankle, and a sports jacket I bought from Cecil Gee. I'd purchased a Dacron white shirt at Marks & Spencer. And a dark blue tie with red stripes. I bought my low-cost brown moccasins from a Bata Shoe Shop in Guyana; they looked stylish but had visible wear.

I was glad to go with a male friend. It enhanced my self-esteem in pursuing dance under the magnificent glow of dazzling light from the ceiling. The men outnumbered the women. According to Fred, some men of colour were smooth operators. He reminded me that positive thinking is the key to success, especially in competition.

The ladies came from various countries, though the English outnumbered the lot. Who were all those ladies? The question came from my inner voice. I related it to Fred.

"Oh, they're generally from the European continent: Austria, France, Germany, Italy, Iceland, Liechtenstein, Scandinavia, Switzerland. Mostly they came to London as au pairs, in a child-care capacity, while learning or improving their English. Avoid women from Iceland: they have an ethnic attitude toward men of colour. A waste of time." He added: "That's why I brought you here. The women are likely to be your "speed": genuine and rarely sophisticated, not in Maggie's league. Don't be surprised if you encounter a few like Maggie!" Fred laughed.

I laughed too. *To each his own*, I thought but said I understood.

"Different strokes for different folks!" said Fred.

"Absolutely."

That evening, I was in the mood to dance and dance. My dancing partners were mostly polite. Few shook heads or looked the other way at my invitation to dance. It was a woman's prerogative. I attempted to have light chats while dancing about London's weather, sights, landscapes, and respective countries. Some of my dancing partners seemed pleased to reply to my questions, while others asked: How long have you been in London? What brought you there? Their curiosity encouraged me to promote myself. I was even motivated to flatter and let my humour shine – ignoring Fred's advice about learning more about the woman.

In the evening, I found myself dancing with a French girl who did not appear chatty but gave the impression that she was interested in what I had to say. Her face was beautiful, and her eyes were a deep, rich brown. I asked her and got her phone number and promised to call soon. Her name was Natalie, and she was from Marseille, France. I chose to be my usual self, not wanting to employ such a ridiculous technique as with Maggie.

After we left the Astoria, Fred performed a slight tease about my cheerfulness. He congratulated me on my "achievement."

"How did you pull it off?" Fred said.

I stated that I was unsure about it. It was all luck, or in part luck, as I joked. It was probably an excellent example of a gentleman's demeanour. We chuckled together. In Guyana, I might have boasted about my triumph to some friends, enabling my ego to proclaim victory. I'd like to think I've matured since then.

I told Fred that I was going to call her the following day.

"Not too soon, man! After all, if she likes you, you don't have to rush things," he said.

His argument didn't sway me. My playing hard to get cost me many an opportunity in Guyana. I told Fred that he was probably right, that appearing overzealous may upset the apple cart.

That night I went to bed, pondered on the evening's happenings and woven into romantic fantasies - dreamlike as in movies - and staged by the heart's longings. I felt cheerful and content and, like a child, wished for happiness and the lack of grief in my life. It shouldn't take much in a person's life to alleviate loneliness. I thought when I gave in to the bosom of slumber.

A few days later, I got a telephone call. It was in the morning, around nine. I wondered who would ring this early. Perhaps it was for Don or Leo, although they rarely rang me. I thought of Fred, but he rarely is up that early. What about the Labour Exchange? Why not? Officials have a way of checking you.

"I called you a few times," said the voice, "You're a busy bee!" It was Sam.

I tried to get what Sam was insinuating.

"No! My time spent searching for work had become a tedious task in the face of what had become a massive challenge. I remained defiant," I said emphatically and without hesitation.

To cut a long tale short, Sam invited me to lunch. I told him that I would get back to him. I pondered: I may inform him after I've got a job. I assumed it would be a way to get him off my back.

I had the feeling that Sam was spying on me. My father was too proud to write to me about whatever it was. Perhaps Sam had informed him about Fred.

I recall my mother writing that I should be wary of the people I associate with and continue to accept the guidance of the Lord. It was lovely and bright for her, a devout Christian. I sometimes struggled to discern the Lord's word from Satan's––whether it came directly to me or through someone else.

My mother knew me: posh people quickly impressed me. It was amusing when someone knew you better than you knew yourself. I wouldn't mind marrying a considerate and gentle woman, understanding and forgiving––a heart full of love and compassion. Is that also the reason for my admiration for older women? A mother's love is unconditional, but a lover's love is not.

I found it hard to be objective about my mother. In childhood and adolescence, I could only consider her, in favourable terms, almost perfect. In my later years, I examined my parents' strengths and weaknesses during the onset of a delayed middle-aged crisis that confronted me. Parents aren't perfect, which sounds like a cliché, though I needed to remind myself there exists no perfection in anybody. Because, from as far back as I could remember, I was prone to idealising some people and flawing others. My parents had become opposites in my imagination and thoughts for whatever reason. I read somewhere that the mental images we have of someone do not precisely correspond to the person in real life.

12
LONDON

FRUSTRATION BEGAN TO surface a few weeks following the interview. Previously, I had been lonely, but that was no longer the case because I had hopes for the French girl. But I remained wary. There was no certainty that I would find satisfaction and fulfilment in some crucial areas of my life. I'm thinking about a love relationship and work.

I hadn't heard from Miss O'Connor, the assistant personnel officer, for two weeks after the job interview at Bailey's Aero & Rubber Co.

One evening in the flat at home, I mentioned my bleak situation of not having a job.

"I'm surprised you haven't got an answer there and then, the custom with low-rated employment," Don remarked:

"I was one of several applicants," I retorted. "These are desperate times for unskilled labour," feeling nauseated by the reality.

"Surprise her! Miss Whatever-her-name! Give her a call!" Leo said.

"Nay, I already feel like a prick, begging for handouts," I said.

"Then take it on the chin and move on," Don agreed.

"Perhaps I should do one or the other: ring up or ignore," I said.

While pondering, I figured Miss O'Connor's joviality had given me optimism about gaining the job. However, my experience has taught me not to take things for granted. The overwhelming guidance I received from my GP, the official of the Labour Exchange (who visited the house), the Lutheran priest, and Fred seemed to encourage me to hold on to a positive perspective." It was, however, beginning to sound like a cliché because my negative beliefs were receiving nourishment from first-hand experiences.

I had planned to call Miss O'Connor and give her a piece of my mind for taking so long to respond, but I never did.

Not until this morning, about 10 a.m. The operator or receptionist informed me she was unavailable and that I might call again later, ideally after 3 p.m. I ignored the operator's request to leave my name and told her it wasn't that essential.

On Tuesday of the following week, I received a letter from Bailey's Aero & Rubber Co. Is it good or bad news? To heck with the job and the letter, I thought to myself.

Nonetheless, my heartbeat accelerated. It felt like a near-panic attack, far worse than when high school exam results were published. I began counting backwards from 1,000 and taking deep breaths simultaneously.

My composure was back. I reread the letter before grasping its contents as if written in a foreign language, or my wits were still adrift. I could then take it all in and couldn't believe my eyes:

Dear Mr Holmes, I am delighted to inform you that you have been chosen to fill the opening in the machine department. You are expected to appear on Monday at 8 a.m. promptly. I'm looking forward to meeting you

Yours respectfully, Mr J. Fitzgerald, the personnel officer at Bailey's Aero & Rubber Co.

I felt a flush in my cheeks. My voice and an echo down the corridor burst in hurray, hurray.

Goodbye to months of a long string of poor luck. I thought of phoning Sam. But on second thought, I considered it best not to rush with such tidings, for there was no genuineness to inform him immediately. I also felt like calling Natalie, not to brag about my new position, but to hear her voice or chat with someone pleasant. Such a spontaneous phone call might not have gone well. Natalie had told me it was "better to call me on my day off, Wednesday or Sunday." I considered dropping by Fred's place. Knocking on his door before 3 pm wouldn't have been fruitful since he was a night owl and rarely answered the door before 6 pm.

Instead, I thought of what to wear to work on Monday. In most situations, first impressions count. I'd wear a pair of blue dungarees and a black jacket that belonged to my serge suit. I would not miss out on shining my brown moccasin for a change. The phrase *any job* came to mind. That was what I became: someone willing to take any job.

13

LONDON

ON WEDNESDAY, I CALLED Natalie on her off day. I didn't have trouble reminding her of who I was, which gave me a pleasant feeling. I asked how she was.

"I'm fine. And you?"

I said I was okay. It was nearly on the tip of my tongue to share the news about my employment. I didn't dare. By being honest, I might have exposed myself to shame. Maybe later, depending on how the friendship developed. I asked Natalie how school was going.

"Oh, it is going good", Natalie said. "Not always, though. Today we wrote a short composition, a shortened version––précis––and conversational exercises."

I asked Natalie what she found most challenging about the English language.

"Oh! Maybe the pronunciation of some words. My French accent gets in the way. Some words are so close to the French and different." She giggled.

I said I didn't have problems understanding her English.

"That's kind of you to say."

"I was wondering if I could invite you somewhere. To the cinema, or maybe to a cosy coffee bar in Earl's Court, or wherever you'd like to go," I said.

Natalie said, "On Sunday, I must meet my friends. Maybe the next Sunday."

"That's fine with me," I said. "Do you want us now to decide on a time and place?"

"We can decide now," she said. "You can choose somewhere to meet. In the afternoon."

I decided to meet Natalie at 2 pm under the Coca-Cola neon sign at Piccadilly Circus, one of my meeting spots for dates.

I felt relieved that the first conversation on the phone went smoothly. A couple of times in London, following a hearty initial meeting, chatting over a cup of tea with a girl, and obtaining her number, then witnessing the whole thing falling apart later. It was different in BG (British Guiana). Some acquaintance with the girl existed before a date.

I remember once meeting a German girl, Hannah. We had agreed to meet in Piccadilly Circus under the Coca-Cola neon sign. I waited for her for a long time. At first, I thought she had missed her north Tube from Uxbridge, Middlesex. Over time, there was still no sign of Hannah. I called her at the family where she worked as an au pair. An older female voice answered, and then Hannah's voice popped up.

So, she was home, I thought. Then I lost my cool before I realised it. My bellicose remarks about her taking a mickey out of me robbed me of my senses. It was as if my rational self wasn't equal to its counterpart.

After I cooled down, I heard Hannah explain she could not reach me by phone. "My lady" (the woman she worked for) had requested her to babysit the kids on her day off with little notice.

I'd messed up! The influence of negative anecdotes from some male acquaintances at the Student Centre, and my impulsive, rude behaviour, had ruined a possible romance with a beautiful young woman. Hannah also seemed charming and genuine. That was something I would never forget. I blamed myself for my impulsiveness and willingness to listen to such negative stories from other men.

14

LONDON

IT WAS MONDAY MORNING. Mr J. Fitzgerald, the personnel officer of Bailey's Products Co., had his office on the third level of the fifth-floor building, escorted me to the ground floor and presented me to my new boss, Saunders.

"Morning," Mr Saunders said solemnly. I greeted him with a "Morning" and a smile.

Mr J. Fitzgerald wished me a good day and left me in the hands of my new boss, in the working-class parlance.

My new boss told me to follow him. I nodded and followed. Mr Saunders wore rimless glasses that made him look like a former schoolteacher. He was wearing a white shirt and grey tie, grey flannel trousers and a white work coat, the length of which was just below the knee. His face was broad, with prominent cheekbones, and his hair was black and oily, reminding me of Brilliantine, which I had used in Guyana. His shoes were flawlessly gleaming.

I childishly fancied the idea of attiring myself in a coat identical to Mr Saunders'. I'd most likely wind up with a blue-overall worker who operated machines (with drills and flow of milky substance). Workers transformed aluminium material into discs of some sort or another. Mr Saunders had given me a tour of the department floor. My designated task was to sweep and dispose of aluminium debris and other fragments from machines powered by men in blue overalls.

Then I went to a location known as the warehouse. A middle-aged English woman stood behind a counter, one of the few who managed requests for objects like tools, bolts, nuts, and the like. I received two brown overalls.

I was instructed when to sweep, which was every hour or so. "Have you done this line of work before?' Mr Saunders asked.

"No, sir, I haven't, but I'm a fast learner," I said.

"That's fine," my foreman said, nodding; his lips carried a slight smile. He reiterated, "Every hour or so," pointing, "from here to there and straight ahead." I estimated the area to be 100 yards long and 50 yards wide. Added to that was an errand-boy duty that fetched orders to and from the storage.

The plant was large, with at least one hundred or more blue-collar employees. The company manufactured various minor aircraft components.

I finally rejoined the British workforce, and my 21st birthday was a few months away.

To avoid the details about my work, I phoned my mother, and, according to her, so was my dad. I pictured my mother praising the Lord in prayer and hymns at church and home. My father, I assumed, would likely express an apologetic remark about me to his drinking buddies. My loving sister Sandra would undoubtedly thank the Lord. Later, I felt compelled to jot down my thoughts about the significant changes in my life.

Out of habit, I continued to thank God, but not as frequently as I used to. It evolved into a sense of duty with some guilt attached. I prayed from time to time before going to bed, although mechanically performed. "The Lord is my Shepherd, I shall not want, He maketh me to lie down in green pastures: he leadeth me beside the still waters. He restoreth my soul. ..."

Praying was a routine or a sense of guilt or fear. A year or two later, praying would be gone from my life.

My weekly earnings would be £10. Not much, when you consider the purchase of a weekly travel ticket, tea breaks and lunches at the personnel canteen, dinner at the Student Centre and the rent. Making a weekly deposit of one pound into my Post Office account would become a habit.

Regardless of the impression I sometimes gave in this chronicle, it seemed preferable to work than to be on the dole or spend idle time with bad company. I would write to friends about attiring myself to a different dress style and eliminating outdated clothing from Guyana. I'd noticed an English bloke doing his rounds in my neighbourhood on certain days with a push or bicycle cart, buying second-hand clothing. I doubt the vendor offered the seller a fair price.

15

LONDON

MY SUNDAY DATE WITH Natalie. We met at Piccadilly Circus and agreed to take a stroll and talk about ourselves. She was a pretty woman. Her face was more attractive than I remembered, with brown eyes, a slender nose, and thin and thick lips that first caught my attention (because my lips were a similar size). Her height was average, and she was chubby. Her complexion carried the shade of cream coffee. Her mother was an Afro-French Guianese, and her father was a white Algerian.

I recall a particular pride in being seen with her as we wandered through the area. On my previous dates, girls who were European, some English and one or more West Indians. Some English men had stared at my Caucasian girlfriends. I saw their facial expressions and wondered what they were thinking; some appeared mildly discontented. Being with Natalie, the staring was the same, which I considered peculiar. Was it merely old-fashioned jealousy? In time, I would become oblivious to gazing in such circumstances.

16

LONDON

AS THE WEEKS WENT BY, I carried out my duties as a sweeper/errand boy as best I could. At times, I wore a smile while humming a song perhaps I'd heard on the BBC Radio Breakfast Show hosted by Tony Blackburn. In moments of boredom, I allowed my mind to wander, thinking about the date with Natalie. I tried not to let my mind stray for long. An excellent performance was imperative to maintain if you were a new boy.

Then in three months, I became dissatisfied with my occupation. The dullness stifled me as the appreciation disappeared. I now wanted something better.

I felt powerless and prayed out of desperation and despair because mental and emotional agony was excruciating. I cursed myself. I moaned about the situation in which I had placed myself. Was such an occupation still preferable to being on the dole?

It remained dignified to have any job than to live on the backs of multitudes. Even so, I could not help becoming miserable. My positive frame of mind was out of function. To be vain was to be sinful. I ought to be thankful for small mercies, but I could no longer be thankful.

I couldn't vent to Sam, Don, or Leo. None of them would understand. They would only remind me that the best way to escape menial occupations was to pursue a proper profession, which required three or more years of study.

So, I turned to Fred, and he understood.

"Such jobs only catch those desperate or have no other option," he said. "It'd be enough to send me into a tailspin. Life is full of monotonous jobs."

I agreed and thought of millions of poor folks in Africa, India and South America in menial labour who probably had no time to complain. I wondered who in hell had invented work, or had the reason been to keep boredom at bay?

Irrational or nonsensical thoughts come into my mind as alternatives: to quit the job without notice and return to unemployment in exchange for financial support.

What about becoming a hustler, living by my wits? Or to write my mum for sympathy and a return fare?

None of which appealed to me.

I had to do something. I could not continue month after month in that dummy of a job. To hell with the idea of Sam: *the newcomer to the motherland must take whatever job from the start*. I did not like his modesty. A beggar's rationale! I wanted things my way, and begging wasn't one of them. True, some compromises, though not too many, not overdoing it! Anything above the rank of a sweeper.

I shared such thoughts with Fred, who merely looked away, smiling. Then he said: "I once told you to use for your wits in the white man's world. Black people must find alternative ways to survive without higher education and a disposition that does not work well with regular 8-5 work.

I thought of giving up my job or feigning physical pain because I wanted the GP to prescribe lighter duties, which would not have worked in my favour. It was a gamble but one worth taking. Was it a plan from the devil himself, or did God prompt it through my mother's constant prayers to the Almighty Lord?

Then something happened, and I wasn't sure what it entailed, whether to aggravate or improve my situation.

17

LONDON

AFTER LUNCH ONE DAY, my foreman Mr Saunders informed me that I had to work in another department for an hour or two. I went to this department expecting to find a similar task because I had my broom with me. To my surprise, the job was to lay out tiny metal objects, like links, on twelve-by-twelve-inch cardboard sheets. The items seemed like thousands, lying in a wooden crate. I inquired with the boss in that department whether there was a time frame attached to the work. "Oh, no!" laughed Mr Firestone, the assistant foreman. "Do as much as you can with the time you have."

I didn't mind, even if it meant spending the rest of the afternoon there. That was okay with me. The activity proved to be simple, requiring just a modicum of concentration.

I remember talking to a fellow sweeper/labourer from that department during a tea break in the canteen. This grey-haired Irish man smoked a lot and frequently chatted with others. He and I struck up a conversation.

"I don't mind the job, don't mind at all," the Irish man, who introduced himself as Smithy from Cork County, Ireland, said. "I usually take a few breaks to place bets at the bookmakers," I asked what he thought about working here and mentioned that I found it tedious.

I then asked him about Smithy's time with the company.

"15 years. You're young! As we say in Ireland: *Everything will be all right. Suppose it's not all right. It's not the end.*"

"In Guyana, we say: *good things come to those who wait!* I added my favourite: *God helps those who help themselves.*"

"*What is for you will not pass you by.* Most of the sayings are mainly for a laugh," Smithy said, adding, "I've been playing the horses for decades; I haven't won much: 50 quid the most!"

"I know a few people who spent much time studying the horses and never winning," I said.

"Going back to your previous complaint," Smithy said, "I'd advise you not to overwork yourself. Save your energy for when a better opportunity comes along. I'm getting on; looking forward to retirement, and hopefully, there'll be no redundancy before that." He laughed.

"I'll keep your advice in mind," I said.

"Pretending to be busy, particularly when potential customers appear. It gives the impression of diligence. The 'guv' is easy-going, but the assistant can sometimes drive you up the creek. Getting a pay rise in this company is slow. And the union: collective bargaining is a joke!"

"Good to know," I said, smiling. I carried on with the new task. It was a pleasure speaking with Smithy, the Irishman. One thing was clear: we all have our problems. Instead of lamenting my own, I must remind myself that I'm not the only one with problems.

Most work would be monotonous. I recall thinking about it after seeing photographs of happy farm labourers in Peru, where pay presumably barely covered the cost of living. They may have been singing or cracking jokes. It was the same in Guyana and other countries.

That afternoon's work went quickly and ended there that day. The change of routine or the friendlier atmosphere was probably good for me. Mr Saunders seemed distant and unapproachable. I seemed to function better in a lively environment, which was probably true for most individuals. I sensed indifference from some workers who handled machines.

I couldn't possibly like everyone; therefore, I should understand that others may not like me. It was challenging to feel comfortable in a group setting in which indifference was prevalent.

I coped with the discomfort (a sense of inadequacy) by picturing myself in the company of Natalie, my mother, Sandra, and others.

Later in life, I tackled the situation with unconcern, mirroring the image of a narcissist. I would have read somewhere about the narcissist's projected false self, a defence against depression.

My task in Mr Firestone's department continued, and I immensely enjoyed myself. I discovered that human or animal bodies and inanimate items were x-rayed. I became intrigued by the procedure. Then the inspiration struck to request a transfer. I'd contact Mr Firestone since I had nothing to lose. I aspired to become an industrial x-ray photographer. The dream started.

Six months later, I was hired as an operator in the company's x-ray department. I couldn't have been happier. In my opinion, I maintained my standing as somebody in English society. I'd worked my way up from collecting unemployment benefits to becoming a sweeper/labourer and an industrial x-ray operator.

It felt significant at the time. I wore a white overall, but occupational standing remained that of a blue-collar worker in the canteen where there was a division of ranks.

18

LONDON

WITH ITS BARRENNESS, chill, and snow, winter arrived, stunning the country and me with massive snowfalls and days of sub-zero temperatures. The press made a huge thing of it, reporting about stoppages at various factories around the country because of the chaos on the roads and railway lines and damaged and frozen water pipes. The media criticised the Conservative administration for its handling of the situation. Such weather has not been seen in the United Kingdom for many years.

If I recall correctly, the English frequently grumble about the weather, unlike Guyana. With much snow and frost, the country had enough about which to complain.

The heavy snowstorm had arrived one evening while I was indoors: the snow fell on rooftops and windowsills, giving the roads and streets, parked vehicles, and the ground a great appearance from my single window. After lighting the modest gas heater at the hearth for an hour, my room felt warm and cosy. It was my first sight of snow, and the thought made me proud that I (rather than my pals in Guyana) was seeing winter conditions.

After leaving the flat in the morning rush hour, the snow soon got into my shoes. I fought through the heavy snow on the sidewalks to a bus stop and Underground Station. The roads were chaotic, with enormous traffic bottlenecks and delays. I suddenly became one of a pitiful bunch.

When the alarm started buzzing, I had to leap out of bed in the frigid bedroom, put on the heater, and then go back under the covers until the room warmed up.

It took a long time to get to work on time. Buses and trains struggled to adhere to schedules. I never wanted to miss a workday due to inclement weather, only when I got a bad cold with sneezing and fever. My absence from work cost me a chunk of my pay for the first two days.

My tonsils began to bother me after I moved to the UK. I'd never experienced such problems previously and believed it was due to the London fog and environment. Soot was always on my white handkerchief.

The cold weather affected my hands and feet. And the pair of gloves I got from our landlord, Mr Linton, in Guyana, I forgot them in a Wimpy Bar near Earl's Court Underground Station.

I invested in a pair of winter boots but only used them when it snowed. A London university woolly scarf became handy. But the Victorian winter coat from Mr Linton was heavy.

My boss praised me for how hard I worked and how rarely I was absent.

I had my first birthday in Britain. My parents and siblings had sent me greetings, a £10 check, and a card or two from friends. The cards brought a mixture of nostalgia and sadness. I imagined what a lovely party it would have been: my mum's delicious cake, my dad providing maybe intoxicating beverages (rum and coke-cola), and my friends and a few of Sandra's; and making me feel cheerful, entertaining the idea of having a place in their heart. Oh! The memory had made me wish I were in Guyana–at least for my twenty-first birthday.

Whatever the melancholy, Natalie invited me to the cinema to see "Vivre Sa Vie," a film by French director Jean-Luc Godard. It was subtitled, which was a blessing. It was a story about a woman who dreamed of a better life; she married, but her marriage was unhappy, so she returned to a life of prostitution. The end was tragic. Art was imitating life, I remember thinking.

The more one talks, the less the words carry meaning – a line from the movie that stays with me for some time.

Natalie had so wanted to watch the movie. It was my day, but I chose to be generous. My mum would have been proud of her son. Natalie had, at last, decided to stay the night.

19

LONDON

THEN THE CHRISTMAS season arrived, and I longed for my family. I was alone because Natalie had gone to her parents. My mum sent me a lovely black cake, money, a gold ring, and a cute card depicting my first steps––but all that could not prevent sadness. The tears welled in my eyes. I was sentimental about Christmas; it had a certain romance about it.

After the age of 45, my feelings for the season would fade. The season became another time to drink, eat and be merry, minus sentimentality.

I listened to Nate King Cole and Johnny Mathis's favourite songs on my record player that first Christmas. I wasn't alone in the flat; Don and Leo were also there. We felt deprived of the company of girlfriends. London streets appeared deserted. It was as if many English people were visiting relatives in other parts of the UK. Or they travelled to warmer destinations such as Spain or the Caribbean, leaving the town for tourists and lonely souls, like the three black men in a Chelsea apartment.

Sam invited me to his home on Boxing Day: he had a few friends over for a "get-together." His wife Daphne had gone to Guyana for the holiday season. I showed my respect by attending. I didn't want to upset my parents.

On New Year's Eve, Fred invited me to a party. I was overjoyed for such a night since I didn't want to spend time with my flatmates watching TV. I was sentimental about the last night of the year; I always hoped for something better from the new year.

On the other hand, my new year's resolutions never survived the test of time. My obstinate habits remained my foe, an exhausting effort that seemed ridiculously hopeless, with me in Sisyphus' sandals.

Fred wore a maroon tuxedo, a white shirt with double cuffs, a black bowtie, maroon trousers, and Gucci 1953 Horse leather shoes. I donned Leo's black tuxedo, a white shirt with cuffs, a black bowtie, black slacks, and a second-hand pair of black shoes.

The party was in Bayswater, and Thursday, the hostess, was tall, thin, with ginger hair and freckled. She probably was in her mid-forties and owned an antique boutique in Knightsbridge. Fred had met her a year before in a pub in High Street, Kensington.

Thursday (named perhaps after the Norse God of thunder; no doubt a reflection of her father's vanity) appeared delighted to have Fred and me there. She gave a joyful cry as she greeted us with a tight embrace and a kiss on the cheeks in the French style.

I envy Fred at the time. I didn't mind getting emotionally entangled with Thursday, but I sensed I wasn't up to the mark. Of course, Natalie was sweet, calm, and shy and probably suited me. I was impulsive in matters of romance. As a young man, I hoped the habit would disappear with age and maturity would take over. Alas! My adulthood was undoubtedly interrupted by the punishment of the gods.

Thursday had *class* while Natalie was a sweet bird from pastoral life. Natalie had a certain innocence, generosity, and sincerity. Thursday was (according to Fred) a serpent in disguise.

Why do I fall for dubious types or *damaged goods*?" I regarded myself in similar terms. The Thursdays of this world appeared "vulnerable," requiring love and affection. Probably it had something to do with a projection—my social mobility agenda. In Guyana, I pursued a similar passion, admiring women from higher social strata, even though I had nothing to offer them except my false pride and youth.

What does it matter? Whatever! That night at the party, I had the impression that I was in the right place. The self-destructive person I appeared to be.

I was impressed by what I envisioned Thursday and her stylish pad: carpeting, antique furniture, central heating, artwork, and the like. Did she own the flat or rent it?

It didn't matter.

I asked Fred: "Where could I meet women like Thursday? What does it take? Wealth, I suppose. What about my youth?"

Fred smiled his customary serene smile. "In Guyana, you need money, like a *big shot* (someone belonging to high society). If you play your cards right, style and tact can be significant assets in London. It sounded simple, but not everybody had style and subtlety! You either have it or don't."

So, it wasn't about being wealthy or a youth. Good-looking and rich people may rarely be impressed by others' wealth and beauty. It sounded simple: style and subtlety—Fred's idea.

Fred added, "It's more to do with the character. It cannot be bought or taught."

As if gifted with a charismatic personality, I reasoned. It remained mystical to me: style and subtlety.

I attempted to imitate Fred's manner and subtlety when the party got going. I took some alcohol to maintain my wavering self-esteem. I would approach women of all types. Being like Fred, I would discover it wasn't all that simple. Women of "class" appeared versed in arts and literature and had a posh accent. All I had going was mainly my Guyanese humour and folktales and my high school knowledge of British literature. Perhaps being oneself was the key; the thought suddenly appeared to me: I was trying hard to be like others. I decided there was no need to imitate Fred.

I found myself standing alone, with a drink and a cigarette, watching Fred in his element––his dancing, chatting, and hearty laughter. I thought of Jay Gatsby. Could Fred be compared to a Guyanese Gatsby, a mystery person, or Lucky Gordon, a Jamaican jazz singer? During the Profumo Affair in the new year, Lucky Gordon became renowned.

The thought that I lacked style and subtlety affected my self-esteem. I imagined everybody had noticed I didn't have those two vital qualities.

I took a double brandy to support the evening's challenge, and I had my old pals in Guyana in my thoughts. I imagined the envy in their hearts when I sent them news of this classy New Year's Eve party. Don't mess things up, Harry! I whispered to myself: The moment was for the taking! I went out in quest of a dancing partner, and surprisingly, things got off to a good start.

Another surprise was a sudden change of music: Calypso music of King Fighter. I couldn't ask for more, for luck was on my side. I danced and gobbled down a glass of red wine in the ambience of happiness: the frolicking and exuberance in the delightful music – for I felt like I was in Guyana. I showed the crowd a blend of Guyanese style but no tact attached to Fred's. I decided to mimic a sexy dance style most popular amongst ordinary folks in Guyana, referred to as the "wine," a free-spirited type of dancing, with half-bended knees and rotating the hips in a circular, rhythmic manner, fast and slow.

I then proposed the limbo dance, performing it with an imaginary pole. I was surprised at how well it all worked because everyone followed suit.

There was much applause at the end of *my little show*. Even Fred seemed impressed. I, a new boy, had what it took to catch the attention of "persons of class," as I saw it, by attempting my natural brand of style minus the tact. I did get my sorrowful backside going! The euphoria remained with me. I won a woman's heart through the night before I began to feel like I was about to ––

The next thing I remember was lying on a sofa with a floral pattern. Did anyone talk, or was it a song from a loudspeaker? My eyes opened, and I saw a woman spinning around. I closed my eyes to relieve my nausea. My mind swayed.

As it turned out, hours later, someone held my hand and stroked my forehead. I opened my eyes and saw a woman with black hair and blue eyes. Her voice sounded cheerful, with an accent that sounded familiar. She said: "You've been out for a while. Maybe you've had one too many!"

"I suppose I did, and rapidly," I heard myself say. "Not accustomed to drinking regularly. The heat might have been a factor."

"I'm Catherine, remember me?" She smiled.

"Not sure I do. I'm Harry, a friend of Fred's."

"I know and that you only met Thursday last evening!"

"Thursday? By the way, where am I?" I heard laughter in the distance.

"Still here at Thursday's. She sent me to fetch you. Do you wish for a cup of tea, or would you prefer coffee or a Bloody Mary?" She giggled.

"Thank you, no. What time is it?"

"Morning. Some of us haven't hit the sack yet!" Catherine chuckled.

"Oh, my! I must have missed out on the midnight celebrations."

"That's wretched! We sang and drank to the New Year!" She smirked.

"What a shame!"

Catherine smiled. "Indeed, what a shame.

Following a pause, she said, "May I ask: are you also a musician? I do work in a theatre as an understudy."

"Also?" I asked.

"Well, you danced like a professional jazz ballet dancer."

"Really? I danced the way my countrymen do."

"You certainly fooled me!" She smiled.

"I'm not a musician. I'm afraid—nothing except playing the gramophone. I earn a living in a factory. I x-ray objects."

I thought of Fred's adage: style and subtlety. However, I couldn't be bothered. I was conscious of my speech, mimicking hers a bit. I wasn't making fun of her: I liked RP English.

In my school days, I fancied the idea of winning a Guyana scholarship choosing an Oxbridge college and becoming another person. It remained a fantasy, and I thank the Lord, for I might've become a super snob!

"How exciting, x-raying stuff! Have you done a human being too?"

"Not yet!" I laughed. "I've only been doing it for a short time. What sort of acting do you do?"

"At West End Theatres. I do stand-ins. You know, in case of illness and the like. I may switch later to television, a better means of earning a decent living, though a more competitive branch."

"I haven't been to the theatre. I'm a movie guy."

"Perhaps, you should! Give me your number, and one day I may surprise you with complimentary tickets for you and a loved one or friend."

I said that sounded impressive and thanked her. She seemed a sweet soul, though you can never tell the stereotypical view of their Bohemian lifestyles with actors and actresses.

Catherine and I headed to the kitchen. The hostess and a few men and women friends sat around a table with teacups and looked fatigued. Fred was there, looking haggard.

Fred and I took a taxi home. He settled the bill, which was generous, and I thanked him. He always had loads of cash, a hundred or more pounds, on him. Not bad, I thought. I had two pounds, the most on most occasions. I had more in my Post Office account, though. The lesson my mother taught me had become a virtue.

Yes, I thought I had missed the birth of the New Year, which I would lament over my overindulgence. There was a virtue in showing restraint, and I overstepped the mark. I couldn't hold my drinks. I wanted to be different from my father in that respect and others. The way things turned out in my life, I was no better than him.

Fred recalled the way things were before I passed out. He said he noticed me stealing a few kisses here and there, "in advance" of the impending New Year, and not too long before I passed out. I missed the moment by a few minutes; we all had been waiting for the clock on the wall to strike twelve.

Fred related further: "I noticed you disappeared into Thursday's writing room with the blonde chick who came this morning to fetch you."

"Catherine?"

"Yes, that's her name. It had been Catherine who drew my attention to your plight. Luckily you passed out on a sofa and not on the floor." Fred smiled, perhaps with tiredness. He added that he had helped stretch me out on the sofa and had taken my shoes off. Thursday lent him a pink blanket. He reiterated, chuckling a little, that I must have slipped into slumber with a bellyful of kisses before the strike of midnight.

I smiled at Fred's depiction of the moment, which my memory had failed to capture. All I had was a second-hand account, which was better than none. He also mentioned the music change to Calypso, which had been his doing.

LATER I WOULD WRITE to friends in Guyana about the glorious party with attractive women of class. Also, my humour though a clumsy display of manhood.

I reflected on the party crowd. They may have come from an upper-middle or upper-class or were merely middle or working-class individuals with cultivated attitudes and dispositions intended to mimic an upper-class Bohemian group.

Whatever the reason, it was a new experience for me. I especially liked everyone's manner and style, though hardly original. The highbrow of it all: teasing playfully and mischievously, like kids! I shouldn't be too hard on myself: life seems to turn us into imitating beings.

Why would I desire to be part of such a crowd in Heaven's name? In Guyana, I had friends from well-known families and friends from the middle-class and working-class. To us, whatever social class did not matter. I had a secret admiration for folks from prominent families. My dad, too, though overtly, admired them. He wasn't content with who he was, and I - his son - seemed to be treading in his footsteps.

I cannot remember holding prejudices of class or ethnicity in Guyana because the feeling of mixing with both the socially desirable and undesirable was seldom a problem. I complained about the difference between classes in England, but I needed to figure out where I stood. Like so many, I compared myself to others, one way or another and from habit. I had, however, become aware of my prejudices about class and race. The British might have made me aware of them.

I became discontented, not about my work but my life in general. I felt frustrated and confused. I now wanted to attach myself to some social group. I suddenly wanted to belong, no longer an individual, an outsider. Was I born with a restless disposition, or was my upbringing responsible?

The experiment or the quest for authenticity continued. I began to contemplate the image of being someone who paid little or no attention to the significance of class. The Bohemian lifestyle might have gotten to me.

My model was the individual who had an attractive accent and behaved like a leftish pseudo-intellectual. He would be a reader who spouted opinions found in liberal newspapers like the Guardian and the Observer, and occasionally The News of The World, and periodicals like the leftish New Statesman.

Since my ancestors were enslaved, I still held mixed emotions: anger and shame. In my thoughts, I would sometimes condemn Don, Leo, or Sam, regarding them as mimicking men of the middle-class Englishman. In retrospect, I was a copycat, though a wild type.

Fred wasn't like Don or Leo or Sam, though his clandestine manner made him too much of a mystic to me. I admired his calm and collected way, never impulsive behaviour or overindulgence. Always in control of himself! I figured that he was much too smooth to be genuine. There probably was no mystery to him: Fred might've modelled himself on a Hollywood male figure from the 40s. Of course, that's sheer speculation. Who can safely say what drives people to fashion themselves after someone else? My desire for self-realisation would gradually cease.

20

LONDON

DESPITE THE CHILL, the freshness of another spring gave me an incredible sensation. Soon, flowers will open, leaves will emerge, and grass will become green. Once again, you'll hear birds singing and see them soaring. As a kid, I was used to this, and I admit I could have taken it for granted.

What, if anything, did I learn that I wouldn't have gotten in Guyana? There were downsides to life abroad, to be sure, but there were also benefits. Regrettably, I did not hold myself in high regard for hastily abandoning my homeland. I vowed to be more rational the next time I faced a decision of this nature—my tendency to act impulsively caused issues.

Regarding my physical appearance, I was still a tiny person. However, it didn't surprise me that my stomach muscles were relatively strong. But by the time I was twenty-five, I was bloated from eating Italian lunches daily. My height remained the same at 5 feet 8 inches, and too early in age to be shorter.

There came the point where I was willing to accept the idea that I was growing up. I had taken a step towards independence by leaving Don and Leo's Chelsea flat and moving into my place. I'd found a little room on Old Brompton Road, within walking distance of the Student Centre. It was one of my new year's resolutions: to find a place again to call my own.

Now that I didn't have roommates, Natalie seemed more open to staying over. I told her about the New Year's Eve party but omitted the details. She was glad, for my sake, for having had precious time. She had gotten used to my sad moods. At last, I started to cook, partly to impress her and for my sake. Another step towards self-reliance and another New Year's resolution. She enjoyed the Caribbean cuisines I had prepared. They were the ones I had liked while growing up. I was still a fussy eater.

I wanted to stop consulting friends or acquaintances for advice before making decisions. But it appeared easier said than done. I made an exception by calling Fred, but his telephone seemed out of order. I went to his pad to discover that he had moved. Bloody hell! I felt agitated and hurt. I had spoken to him days before – not a word nor whisper. I sought his favourite pubs and bars.

Where was my mentor, my friend? I sought the opinions of others who knew him. Recently, no one saw him. His disappearance was speculated upon by several. It may have seemed odd that he didn't inform anyone he had to be invisible for a time, but he wasn't the kind to avoid trouble by hiding. I didn't know what to make of Fred's disappearance.

Nonetheless, Fred did not bother to tell me. I recall dad telling me not to trust anyone or something to that effect. I felt like I had lost someone I had put my faith in. He was his own man, and he and I didn't come from the same tree.

Moody blues, and slight fear, accompanied me. I coped with those spells without comfort from anyone, including Natalie. I was ashamed of my troubles and regarded them as a sign of weakness. Later I discovered that wasn't the case, and I learned to accept it as part of who I was. I learned to deal with panic attacks as best I could, usually without the help of medication or alcohol. I stopped expressing such issues to my mother and sister, Sandra, to avoid bothering them.

In the remaining weeks of spring, I went to work dressed in a sports jacket with leather patches at the elbows. I wore light-brown Manchester trousers, brown suede boots, and a black-tie diagonal stripe. I picked up a copy of The Guardian at Earl's Court Station, took the District Line to Edgware Road Station, and read the newspaper. Later I stopped for a few minutes at the café to buy two cheese sandwiches.

Reading the Guardian was done with ostentation as if to proclaim, "Look here! I'm not just another ordinary immigrant; I'm different from the herd, intelligent, literate, cultural, well-mannered, and a respectable family. Does it matter what others think? I have exaggerated it, albeit out of the need to be recognised in society.

Looking back, I expected too much from Guyana and England. In time, I would limit my expectations and appreciation to a few friends, acquaintances, and books.

On Monday morning at work, some bloke noticed my new appearance as I made my way to the men's locker room. He was a small, lean worker, probably from the department where I started as a sweeper. He commented about my appearance in jest to some workers who stood by. The comment got under my skin. I bit my lower lip and wanted to seize the moment, and for what? In a fit of madness? Who knows? I stopped, turned around and looked him in the eye; his face wore a mischievous smile. I smiled at the thought of regarding him as a waste of space as I strolled away, cursing him in my mind.

Later I recognised him: an alien from Eastern Europe. Some of them were worse than the British at being racially biased. That was the time I wished I were Bruce Lee.

Unfortunately, I am a frail, black sparrow. The brute force would have served me well. I would have lost my job and more and become a bigger fool. Growing up, I had witnessed men who lost their self-control and committed despicable crimes for vanity's sake in a moment of anger.

Someone at work once remarked I had a chip on my shoulder. If that were the case, I would have to free myself from the burden. I should learn how men of noble disposition treat fools.

In Guyana, one of my friends gave the impression that he was better than most. Other friends and I made fun of him. We nicknamed him "Billy the highbrow." Surprisingly, he wasn't offended. Coolness was his middle name. Sometimes I would think of Billy's laid-back style and hope some of it rubbed off on me by taking a page from Billy Butt's book. I would, however, remain light years away from the art of suffering fools gladly, especially for minor grievances.

I moved to Penywern Road in Earl's Court at the start of summer, where I got a better single room. The rent was a bit higher, but I also liked living there. The *bad apples* still live on Cromwell Road, but we rarely cross paths. I was still within walking distance of the Student Centre.

I bought a radio/record player and three jazz LPs: thirty shillings each, not cheap. Bill Evans, Dave Brubeck Quartet, George Shearing, and Jimmy Smith. I was more interested in modern jazz. I met another Jamaican student, Wilfred, who introduced me to Miles Davis's Porgy and Bess, which was first released in 1959. In Guyana, my first jazz LP was But Not for Me by Ahmad Jamal Trio, bought in 1961.

21

LONDON

CATHERINE CALLED AT work to ask for my address to send me two free tickets. I politely insisted on inviting her for a drink in return. I added that I was curious to know more about her acting career. After some hesitation, Catherine agreed to meet me.

One Friday after work, we met at The Cambridge pub on Charing Cross Road, near the Palace Theatre on Shaftesbury Avenue. We greeted each other with a hello and a hug. I never had a date in Guyana in a pub, but it was a custom in England to which I quickly got used.

"Nice to meet you, Catherine!"

"Nice of you to invite me for a drink."

"What can I get you, love? I'm going for a beer. My regular treat to myself at the end of each workweek." I laughed.

"I'll have a beer too, but the medium size. I'm working tomorrow."

"At the weekend?" I asked.

"It's like that in my profession. I've got used to it."

I asked about her acting, which began at school. She grew up in Sussex, a rural county in southeast England. I was once on a day trip to Brighton but didn't mention it. I asked her about her private life and if she had a boyfriend or boyfriends because I wanted to meet her.

She exclaimed, "Ha-ha, I was expecting that!" She added, "Well, I have a boyfriend, but he's in a relationship which will end."

"Sounds like a love triangle. I suppose the guy is married."

"Oh no, but they've been together for two years, and he wants to end it. They have their ups and downs. She's been seeing somebody else but broke it off. It's complicated, but he and I go well together."

"That sounds groovy! I arrive too late in the lives of many women."

She smirked. "Don't say that! You're a sweet, cheerful guy. Miss Right will one day show up!

We can continue to meet, but only as friends."

"I'm not all that pleasant as some people believe. If necessary, I can be your friend: a shoulder to cry on." I smiled.

"That would be nice. I find it natural to chat with you."

Catherine and I had agreed on a friendship. Luckily, the situation could change for the better or stay that way. Even if it didn't work out for her, the best friends could become a couple, though not in my experience. Getting to know each other too well wasn't the ideal way to become a couple.

Catherine and I would meet once a month for a friendly chat over a beer, acquainting myself with plays, the novels she read, and what went on behind the scenes with well-known actors. Her triangle problem of love remained afloat. I figured she wasn't going to give up on her lover. It didn't worry me, though, for I'd gotten used to our friendship. Having such a girlfriend had its merit in Guyana. I always appreciated some women as friends to trust, better than men.

BEFORE NATALIE FINALLY returned to France, I used the two tickets I had received from Catherine for the musical hit "Half a Sixpence" at the Cambridge Theatre in Covent Garden. It was from the Kipps novel written by H. G. Wells. "A salesman in a cocktail shop inherits money and is torn between his childhood love and society." According to a review in the Guardian, *the clunky plot is there to set off a comic parable about social mobility or its absence.*

I remember coming out of the play that I enjoyed tremendously. It made me think of my social mobility, which wasn't strange or unnatural, as some of my rotten apple friends would probably regard it. They had little or no ambition, apart from living like thieves. In retrospect, I wanted too much and was impatient with life.

22

LONDON

AFTER NATALIE LEFT, I started experiencing mood swings for a few days. Usually, when I was alone and had nothing but memories. I would wake up feeling like I had lost a real love affair, the best I had ever had. I wouldn't claim it was perfect, but it worked for someone as neurotic as me. I wasn't sure whether Natalie felt the same way; I could only assume her feelings for me were on par with mine. Most of the time we were together, we got on well. We discussed our understanding of love, likes and dislikes, goals for the future, etc. We talked about the meaning of life, human existence, the struggle between good and evil, our illusions and more. We were both philosophical and psychologically inclined. We didn't always agree on everything, which we understood and respected. Sometimes she was silent, while I was talkative; it was the other way around on different occasions. It wasn't a problem.

We enjoyed each other's humour, and we laughed a lot together. We went to the cinema and took walks in the parks, hand in hand. We would sometimes return to my single room, I would cook something, and she would stay the night.

Natalie wasn't keen on jazz, but she liked Bill Evans's "Peace Piece" and his rendition of "My Foolish Heart." Her favourite music included Edith Piaf, Charles Aznavour, Otis Redding, and Sam Cooke. We occasionally quarrelled over small topics that did not last long.

Then it all – this togetherness – ended, and it was inevitable. We were young and had our future of which to think. Natalie wanted a life in France, and I dreamed of a life in America. She returned to France to study and later work as a social worker. Natalie set her sights on serving dysfunctional teenagers with familial and practical problems. She had a purpose in life, and I lacked a clear vision.

We promised to write and phone regularly. I considered visiting Natalie over the Christmas season in Marseille at her parents' place. If not, then a few days in Paris next summer, where we thought it would be nice to be together. I promised to work on the French she taught me, perhaps through a correspondence course or borrowing tapes from the library. I had fancied the idea of studying French in France as an au pair–whether that was feasible, I would never know.

After Natalie returned to France for months, we kept in touch through letters and an occasional telephone chat. Natalie thought we would be together if it were meant to be, for there would be nothing but death to keep us apart. I told her that might turn out to be the case. I wasn't sure about it, for human lives seemed partly or wholly governed by "accidental happenings."

I tried to stick to the promises that gave credibility to our relationship. Then, when self-doubt took control, the effort would fade, and I'd give in to emotional weakness. Then my promises started to crumble.

During this time, doubts became allies, and the love dream, marriage and family were pushed into oblivion. I found myself with a few women who seemed to love me sincerely, while others wanted nothing more than a short time together.

I became restless with the women who showed me affection, uncertain of what to do with their feelings. I accused myself of being ambivalent, afraid of responsibility, and sceptical of my beliefs and theirs. I felt a passionate desire to have a stable relationship with the women who wanted a causal relationship. In essence, I shied away from emotional involvement.

Where did the notion come from that it was up to you to live a happy life? My life had become complicated and of my own doing. Isn't that the fun—the mix of the foreseen and the unforeseeable, like a roll of the dice? One could not have one without the other. Most essential matters in my life appeared to have happened by chance.

I REMEMBER LUCY, AN English employee. She confided in me about her current affection for a colleague at work. Once I jokingly told Lucy of my desire to seduce the new secretary in our department. Lucy knew this was empty talk because I told her about my low confidence in approaching some women and that I considered myself a flirt for fear of rejection.

Ethel, the new secretary, was English but had lived in Washington, DC, for several years. Ethel was probably twenty years older than me. Since returning from America, she said she shared a flat with her mother in St. John's Wood, which wasn't too far from George Eliot Primary School.

In my usual boyish manner, I would chat Ethel up using my second-hand knowledge from books and romantic nonsense. I held the performance with a smile while my hands sought comfort in my pockets.

I was amazed to find that Ethel had taken my words literally. She surprised me by suggesting that we meet at some point. It was like I couldn't believe my ears. Later, I spoke to her discreetly, offering to take her out for dinner whenever she had the time.

My date with Ethel took place on a Sunday afternoon in late autumn. The autumn weather was windy and rainy, and the trees had lost their leaves. I was on my way to meet her at Sloane Square Tube Station from the upper deck of a double-decker bus.

I took Ethel to a cosy Italian restaurant nearby. We spent most of our time there because of the dreadful weather. I thought about inviting her to my one-bedroom flat. Still, I rejected the idea because I thought it was inappropriate at the time.

On the following date, I promised to cook a Guyanese dinner for her, and she said with a smile, "That sounds lovely."

Lucy pulled something that surprised me: She told Ethel about my intentions, and everything fell through. I was foolish to confide in her about Ethel.

To this day, I have never understood why Lucy did this.

After that, I'd stopped confiding in Lucy about such matters, although she had continued confiding in me. I never confronted her about what she had done. I regarded it as my fault, a lesson not to trust others easily. The Shakespearean quote seems appropriate: Love all, trust a few, and do wrong to none.

Then one day, Ethel went for a drink with some of us at a nearby pub for lunch. She took one too many and then had to go home. She could not manage herself, so our boss asked Lucy and me to drive her home to St. John's Wood. That was the last time Ethel showed up at work. Days later, I called her but received no reply. Then, by chance, she answered one evening. She was naturally embarrassed and apologised for the incident. I said there was no need to apologise because I accused Lucy of encouraging her to drink, which was the case.

After the phone call, I would continue to see Ethel. We became friends and listeners to our life stories. She was Jewish, and we got intimate once. The gods might've provided a helping hand, for she and I lost ourselves in the wilderness of loneliness and despair—poor thing; poor me. I felt sorry for and grieved for our lives, and more than enough to be blue. I shed tears for her and me: we were too fragile human beings; I had the urge, the need to free Ethel from her worries - as unrealistic as in a dream.

For a while, our friendship continued, but our contact would wither in time. I have not forgotten Ethel. She was once a classical pianist, a university lecturer, and the fastest typist I have ever seen.

23

LONDON

THE TIME OF PROTEST: The Washington March had awakened me from a sleep of self-denial, an admission of shame about who I was or pretended to be in England and Guyana. In the media, I read about black protests and violent reactions from law-and-order officials in the USA. I watched it on BBC television at the Student Centre. It was a massive event in black and white.

Before my conscious awakening to the American Dilemma, I'd begun to have mixed emotions for the USA. I felt hostile toward unfair laws and treatment, mainly in this vast country's southern areas. In contrast, my positive feelings for its materialistic lifestyle, glamour, movies, and music industry remained. My overwhelmed affection for the USA was no longer there. I felt an affinity with black Americans, although, at the time, I didn't know a single American. It had to do with them as athletes and singers, and musicians.

While growing up, much white American music beamed from the radio: Perry Como, Patty Page, and Kay Starr. In the later 50s, rock & roll and black artists like Fats Domino, the Platters, Sam Cooke, Johnny Mathis, etc.

In the early 1950s, I remembered American soldiers being in Guyana. They cycled on the pavement, which my schoolmates and I regarded strange because our cyclists rode on the road. I remember seeing a deflated, cream-coloured balloon on the sidewalk and inspecting it briefly with my eyes as I made my way to school. I later learned grownups referred to it as a "French letter," which didn't make sense to a seven-year-old.

A brief television interview in Paris with Afro-American James Baldwin increased my awareness of the black American problem. His fiery eloquence took to me, describing and explaining what it meant to be Black in America. I would eventually read his essays compiled in two books, three of his early novels, and later short stories and plays. I eased up on mimicking English personality figures to boost my self-esteem. I would identify with the Afro-American cause.

In this way, it became my problem: I could not have it both ways. I embraced the radical perspective and rhetoric, airing my opinions with friends and strangers at parties and Speaker's Corner (in Hyde Park, near Marble Arch). The "Black American Problem" and its protests have made me more conscious of my colonial ways. There were occasions when I was radical in thought, and other times my "colonial self" shifted back into mimicking a few Englishmen. Malcolm Muggeridge (British journalist) and David Frost (British television host/ Baron Frost) come to mind. I liked his slow, deliberate, and meticulous manner of speech. The process of imitation went back and forth and was embarrassingly contradictory.

In retrospect, I got tangled up in a web of perspectives, changing spontaneously. It was as if my life had been an empty bubble without a stream of ideas to keep it afloat.

After completing Baldwin's two volumes of essays, I began reading black American protest literature. I drifted closer to his perspective, putting on hold my favourite "white mentors," including Bertrand Russell and Arthur Schopenhauer.

"The black man's burden" had become my new ideology, like a religion or an obsession. I had many discussions with bourgeois-minded West Indians, including Guyanese, and some sympathetic and unsympathetic Brits. As I read black literature, I became more aware of the black man's psychological problems faced in a white environment.

I realised the absurdity of wanting to be someone with middle-class English values and customs, which would lead me further down the path to inauthenticity. Even my au pair girlfriends had the impression I was born in England from my pseudo-British accent, or maybe they compared their English to mine.

In my rounds in bookstores, I would later stumble on Frantz Fanon's "Black Skin, White Masks."

Black literature would produce an inner conflict. I attempted to substitute proper speech with Creole English beyond the confines of the workplace. I read somewhere that a language commits you to (sic) a culture. I began expressing myself in Creole English, but I abandoned the practice.

In retrospect, I took the idea of an authentic black identity to a ridiculous level – too literal, as with religious people and the Bible in Guyana. It reminded me that even James Baldwin's accent was polished.

Because black people's ability to speak English met appraisal in English society, I chose to return to my "cultivated" brand of English.

Years later, I would learn that you couldn't impress your "enemies," which I had been trying to do in England.

As a black person living in a predominantly white environment, I was astounded by the negative impact of racial discrimination and prejudice. I saw myself as an individual in Georgetown (GT), the capital of Guyana.

Later, with Guyana's independence in 1966, national pride permeated the nation's heart. I, an expatriate Guyanese, felt delighted for a brief period, and then my nationalist feelings faded. When I was at odds with white culture, I both envied and detested white and black people for their patriotic impulses.

Few English friends and acquaintances thought I was different from other black people in England. In response, I was able to return the same compliment.

The English atmosphere continued to have an uncontrollable impact on me. My approach to daily life would be pragmatic.

Despite my lack of awareness about negritude, I accepted the ideology of Black Power and its concept of "Black is Beautiful." I did not follow Dr Martin Luther King's passive resistance movement. I took a moderate approach that demanded much faith, hope, and love for all humanity. I had a vendetta against ignorance and stupidity, whether from whites or blacks. I grew into an enraged young black man.

Reading novels by Afro-Americans aided me in discovering my "real identity." In my daily life, society defined me. I believed this was a universal right; everyone could choose their identity.

Depending on my mood, I've attempted to identify my character/personality as an extrovert and an introvert. I might be pleasant or unpleasant. As I can remember, I desired to be respected, but my admiration for others waned or fluctuated.

Decades later, a priest and therapist stated that identity was unchangeable since it consisted of distinguishing characteristics. I choose my perception of myself and how others perceive me. However, I must acknowledge that the therapist (who had had psychoanalytic training) knew what he was talking about.

According to my family tree, some of my ancestors were descendants of enslaved people with a history of miscegenation. I used to call myself a tar baby with silky, wavy hair. I had quadroon buddies with coarse, light-brown hair or ginger hair. My hair and skin tone imply some hanky-panky going on at the time, whether genuine or not. My mother was a quadroon since her grandpa was German, and she knew about my family history. I also saw myself as a "bastard of the West" who was no longer a genuine product of Africa.

I can blame the Western powers, the white race, for all I want. I blame the Moors and Arabs and some West African kingdoms too. I blame "the accident of history." I blame the gods. I blame Satan for misusing his powers. I must accept that "the past is what it is." Others were proud of their heritage, white folks who hadn't been subjected to slavery or colonised.

On the other hand, I--and millions of other lost souls--was still trying to come to grips with the history of the Atlantic Slave Trade and be proud of Africa's history before the birth of a curse.

You didn't have to live in England to understand that "whiteness" wasn't a colour which automatically brought every white person instant opportunity. Many white working-class families were in poverty or, in Guyanese parlance, "catching hell." I remember thinking of their lack of secondary education as one of the numerous factors of their dire conditions.

I was someone of a stigmatised colour. Various ethnic groups (including gipsies) looked down upon persons of black pigmentation. I didn't lack secondary education. I wanted some reasonable explanation for my plight. Self-blame no longer worked.

Regardless, the scenario appeared bewildering. It was full of excuses and denials about racial prejudice and discrimination. Perhaps I should have read a book too quickly and accurately grasp racism. I assumed that for the time being, a layperson's approach would serve, leaving book knowledge for later.

I was thinking about the presence of individuals of colour in the British Civil Service. They might have been emblems (tokens) signifying a lack of discrimination. I couldn't get myself to believe that such biases no longer existed.

Then there was the recruitment of London bus and rail drivers. My case was similar. I rapidly realised that I lacked a convincing foundation for my claim that my problem finding work was due to racial beliefs and attitudes in the mother country.

I didn't always think about my personality as a possible factor. I was tired of finding fault with myself and enduring the consequences. My doctor and the Lutheran pastor have warned me against such an indulgence: "nothing good comes from negative thinking," they say, and their perspective is correct.

I couldn't find a suitable solution after ruling out "poor luck" as probable cause. Reason does not always provide the desired results. It makes no difference what I believe about the why and where of my situation. I softened my stance on pigmentation as a possible explanation for some of my problems in the United Kingdom.

I once dreamed I was a white British working-class bloke and was on "the right side of history" and elevated to incredible heights of social and economic mobility. I had become rich and famous!

There was no grief once I awoke from my dream. Despite my complaints, I understood that my status as a nobody, like billions of others, was not unique in the real world.

I no longer feel that being born with white pigmentation would have improved my life. Nonetheless, whiteness appeared to have the upper hand in culture as firmly ingrained in class, racism, bigotry, and xenophobia as in England. I then learned about the socialist perspective on rank and privilege.

24

LONDON

I KEPT MY JOB AS AN industrial x-ray radiographer. It had lost its glitz and had nothing of which to be proud. Nonetheless, I was fortunate to have a job. The delight and knowledge I got from reading books outweighed the urge to connect with my career. I was grateful for the opportunity to work extra hours. I could immediately pay my bills and deposit funds into my Post Office savings account. I had no intention of looking for another job.

Sandra wrote about her plans to study economics in Canada. She had broken up with her boyfriend and did not go into detail. I was sorry about her sadness and wished her the best of luck. I always disliked the guy. I wanted her to study in England, but Canada was her choice, where she had several friends.

None of my siblings wanted to learn in England, and I couldn't blame them. Thomas and Faye went off to America to study. I seemed to be the only sibling without any plans for the future. I did, however, have a vague idea of pursuing a career. There was no immediate interest in studying. I was content with my undisciplined pursuit of knowledge.

The beauty of learning outside academic institutions' walls was that no exams were involved, so I didn't have to worry about exam anxiety. Most of my compulsory reading consisted of aspects that often bored me, which was what proper education was all about. That may not have been the case with higher education as well.

Sometimes I wondered where my immense interest in reading came from, whether it came from the desire to enrich my self-esteem and well-being. I wish the enthusiasm had begun during my formative years. Better late than never.

Later I would turn to fiction: the novels of D. H. Lawrence, Hermann Hesse (The Glass Bead Game), Thomas Man (Death in Venice), and Dostoyevsky (especially Crime and Punishment and The Idiot).

I remember talking to my Jamaican friend Percival, who was studying engineering. We discussed our future. I had asked him if he would return to Jamaica after his studies.

"Of course, I'm going back home. I only came here to study. What about you, did you come to England to stay?

I smiled, "No, no! Forever would be a living hell! I hope something better turns up."

"A future in this country could be uncertain!"

"I often find life so, perhaps, for most folks." I chuckled.

"What about studying? It would come in handy and maybe cause you to return one day to Guyana."

"I'm not sure about returning to Guyana. Most of my friends are leaving for Canada and America to study."

"Your country is always the right place to be, rich or poor, better than living life as a second-class citizen," Percival said, frowning.

He had a point. For now, that wasn't my choice. "You're right. I'll sleep on it," I laughed.

BOOK THREE

1

LONDON

THE PASSAGE OF TIME did not stop. I still had a job, read a lot, went out, and went on a few dates. One Christmas was spent at Marika's in Amsterdam, while the other was with the family of Ingrid, an au pair girl from Hannover. A few of my Caribbean pals eventually moved back to the Caribbean or left for North America.

A handful of my friends had married, but their unions were already failing. The thought of getting married was always floating around in my head. It looked like a respectable way to live since a family provides security and stability. Like in Guyana, the thought of being a married man and being responsible for providing for my wife and family filled me with dread. On my frail, bony frame, it seemed like an unbearable weight. It was strange to be twenty-four and struggle with wanting a better life without doing anything to make it happen.

I was still figuring out what I wanted out of life. All I had were dreams that seemed impossible to realise. Where did the drive to surpass my father's socioeconomic standing in energy goes? Knowing what I know today, I see that I had set unrealistic expectations for myself and did not put in enough effort to reach my objectives.

My restlessness had returned. I began to consider going back to school. What difference would it make for someone with a restless spirit? While I was in England, I connected with numerous students. The Nigerians were among them. Many tried, but only a few were successful in their lofty goals. They, like many other Afro-Guyanese, aspired to careers in law.

I recall thinking to myself: *I should be ambitious and erase the idea that I was a nobody.* Why not be arrogant and follow the majority? I reasoned. It started to make sense, but I had to overcome my fear of failing. I used to think my life in England was better than my life in Guyana. But there were moments when I felt unsure, such as now.

A training course promised improved skills and paid increases at work became accessible. I decided to apply, and I wasn't the only one interested. A co-worker also showed interest. Mr Patel was able to acquire the course. He was from India and had started in the X-ray department two years before I did.

Mr Patel was a good-natured chap who greeted everyone with a smile. He and I got along reasonably well, despite my irascible temper. He would shy away from conflicts, except those he had with Mr Ali, a Pakistani. Though I kept it to myself, I held a mild resentment about his ingratiating manner towards the bosses.

I remember once when the deputy chief executive, Mr Firestone, was caught in a torrential downpour. In haste, Mr Patel took off, umbrella in hand, to rescue him.

In fairness to Mr Patel, he was a humble fellow who desired to rise above his station. I might have been condescending towards him. Others might have regarded me in a similar light. I was no different to Mr Patel, although our personalities were not the same. Of course, he and I were former British colonials. I had no bad feelings about his promotion. Instead, I blamed myself.

Trying to be objective: I had an attitude. Compared to Mr Patel, I occasionally had heated discussions with the deputy foreman, Mr Firestone, about this or that.

Once I made a significant mistake with a job. I took several erroneous x-ray shots. Mr Firestone suggested I should find another job. Luckily for me, he lacked the authority to fire me. Only Mr McDonald had that power; I had a better relationship with him and was more sympathetic. Mr Firestone wasn't all that bad; he was a cockney with a working-class attitude. Mr McDonald was more of a gentleman.

I had difficulties with a new English colleague who made derogatory remarks about Africa. He worked in Kenya for a year on some British project or another. He had nothing positive to say about his time in Kenya. I never lost my temper with him, of which I was proud. Instead, I spoke to him in a relaxed but firm manner, covered in irony and accompanied by a smile. Later I wasn't happy behaving decently to Jim Bottom's provocations.

I fantasised about rounding up a few *bad apples* to give him a good hiding. I did not because that would have carried things too far. I told Jim Bottom of my astonishment at his banter. It was most unbecoming for someone from the superior race. He retorted by calling me an "African monkey." I smiled and turned away, for I was no match for a nincompoop.

2

LONDON

AFTER LOSING OUT ON that professional opportunity, I was still feeling down. Mr Firestone had shown no support, which was understandable. What stung me the most was Mr McDonald's lack of support. At least, I thought that I got along well with him. Now that I think about it, my high expectations for Mr McDonald could have been unrealistic.

I'd become concerned about one aspect of my personality: my hotheadedness. It wasn't fair to always place the blame on white people. I might have missed out on the training course because of it. I prayed for help but to no avail, as if God wanted me to find a way through His teachings and parables.

In my desperate search for an answer, I read the Bible for clues. I avoided interpreting it literally and came up with a half-baked solution. I would cope with my irascibility before it led to fury by returning to my mother's wisdom, which included the duality of good and evil.

I assumed what Satan's plan was about and thought along the lines of goodness and kindness. Where does a young person find the will to correct a personality defect in the name of God?

I wasn't in control of my life and had no idea what to do. I looked for books for advice without luck. Reading would teach me that my dysfunctional personality was to blame for my tantrums. I developed a positive mentality, accepted flaws, and emphasised positivity in my life. I realised the importance of respecting myself and others.

I had angry thoughts but wasn't always conscious of them. Even in my dreams, I was occasionally upset or furious for no apparent reason. I still feel like a prisoner of my rage, with angry outbursts every few months.

Years later, according to a gruesome handbook on mental diseases, I diagnosed myself with a passive-aggressive personality disorder. In a conversation with the priest/therapist, he wasn't one to label his clientele. Even though the practice seemed widespread, I sometimes imitated mental health experts by applying diagnoses to mark one's enemies.

I STARTED TO ATTEND an evening math class once a week to acquire university entrance qualifications. Maths was part of the essential requirements for university entrance. Studying and reading for leisure still took up much of my free time. Studying mathematics made me feel that my ambition was moving in the right direction.

In retrospect, missing out on the promotion looked like a wake-up call.

Percival, the Jamaican engineering student, would help me. He had a simple way of explaining maths. I was so pleased with the help that I treated him to dinner at an Indian restaurant on Tottenham Court Road.

It would now be a question of choosing a profession or trade. The fear of failure disappeared. Information from a brochure: *Polytechnics provided technical skills and careers for London's workers, industrial skills, general knowledge, health, and well-being of young men and women in the lower classes.*

Reading English and Education are two possibilities for me. It would be part-time because I had to earn a living. Getting a city or local grant to study full-time took a lot of effort. I would take my time and not rush. Enrolling at the College or university level wasn't something to take lightly. I was determined to stay on course and finish it.

Some Caribbean and Guyanese friends did not manage to complete their studies because of economic problems or other issues. Despite their academic excellence, they never received a university diploma, which was regrettable. I used to believe I would strive for the stars if I had their intellect.

Later in life, I learned not to compare myself to others, especially those I felt were more intelligent than me. I also learned that success in life necessitates more than intellectual excellence.

I met a few cool English folks in Oxfordshire through another Jamaican friend, Wilfred. Jane, a single mother of four and a young woman, Alice looked like a young Barbara Streisand. I also met a few English guys with whom I had interesting chats.

I would look forward to the weekends I spend visiting Oxfordshire. By train, it took an hour or more. I didn't mind the time because I always carried a book.

It was nice to meet pleasant English people who helped me dispose of my preconceived notion about English people. Rural people differed from the often-rude English city dwellers. Some argue that our environment moulds us and generates the best or worst in us. I even wanted to move to Oxfordshire. So, I remembered the irony of my last lament about life in my hometown.

It was nice to get away from the Student Centre at weekends. Apart from having dinner there, I read in the library, watched TV, chatted with a few or played ping pong. Once or twice a week, I would shower there.

In Guyana, we used cold showers, which I didn't enjoy. Before jumping under the cold water, I counted from one to three in my teenage years. I never got used to the baths in the English houses I stayed in.

I would strive to control my high expectations of others and myself, which frequently led to disappointments. Setbacks were a normal part of life but having too many was another matter. I recently saw a quote that resonated with me: *Sometimes, we expect more from others because we would be willing to do that much for them.*

I recall reading a newspaper magazine that featured poverty in Manchester or another English county. They were images that worried me but simultaneously reminded me that poverty affected blacks and whites in Britain, Europe, and America.

At times my memory seemed to play tricks, causing me to consider some previous knowledge/experience as new. Nonetheless, it opened my eyes, making me feel less sorry for myself and less colourblind. I had a lot for which to be thankful. My predicament might have been a lot worse. Perhaps it wasn't unusual to assume you were sometimes worse off than others.

3
LONDON

I HAD MICROFILARIA in the late spring of 1965 after being bitten by mosquitoes in Guyana. I became aware of it through a routine blood test associated with my work as an industrial photographer in the X-ray lab at Bailey's Aero Company. I spent a few days at the Hospital for Tropical Diseases in Saint Pancras, London, for routine testing. Treatment consisted of tablets for 6-8 weeks. It was there that I befriended a Swedish nurse, Linnea. We became pen pals, and in one of her letters, she wrote that she would shortly be going to Tanzania to work for one year.

I occasionally ran into a light-skinned and grey-eyed Grenada doctor who came to the Student Centre, maybe for supper and to socialise with other West Indians. Dr Adrian Jones had made regular visits to the South of Sweden. I'm unsure if his excursions are linked to employment or "to play the horses." He was a big fan of horse racing betting. He had good things to say about Sweden. I obtained the phone numbers of a few members of Sweden's "West Indian Diaspora."

I began preparing a brief visit to familiarise myself with black life in Stockholm, the capital. Adrian also gave me three phone numbers of West Indians living in Copenhagen, Denmark. There were also a handful of Guyanese people living there.

"You would like it in Copenhagen," Adrian said. "It's beautiful at any time of the year."

Adrian appeared decent and respectable. We didn't know each other that well. After meeting a Swedish nurse from Stockholm, I told him I'd consider it. I asked him what the distance between Malmö and Stockholm was.

"Six or seven hours by train and just under an hour by plane."

I wrote to Linnea that I planned to visit her country in late December and spend two days in the South and then three days in Stockholm. She suggested I go to The Golden Circle, a jazz club.

4
COPENHAGEN - STOCKHOLM

I TRAVELLED TO SCANDINAVIA just in time to avoid the Christmas season in London. On Christmas Day, I was in Copenhagen, Denmark, and stayed at a reasonably priced hotel. I dialled the three phone numbers Adrian had given me from my hotel room. I was still waiting for a response from two numbers. Then, on the third, fate smiled at me. His name was Henry, and he was a musician and a fellow countryman.

On the phone, he sounded pleasant. He had left Guyana in the 1950s and had lost contact with family or friends. He said, "We could meet for a drink at your hotel, and then you could come to my house to spend time with my family and a few friends."

Amongst tourists, we sat in the hotel lounge. I attempted to provide a hilarious summary of Guyana, but he repeatedly stopped me with disparaging remarks about Guyana. His molars were in full display during his loud laughter. His attention-seeking behaviour had become increasingly embarrassing to me. I got the impression that the beer we were drinking wasn't his first. Henry appeared to have been up all night and looked much older than me, shorter and with a large stomach. I find it tough to pass judgement on anyone at the early phase of acquaintance. Trained psychologists and psychiatrists are said to be adept at this.

More came from Henry, my fellow countryman. In his current state, he drove me to his house while picking up three Danish friends along the way: a male and two women. They showed up as hippies; this was my first meeting with members of the make-love-not-war lifestyle. Henry transported us in one piece to his house.

Then Henry's demeanour shifted: he became critical and condescending toward me. It seemed like I had been changed into a sacrificial lamb on Christmas Day! What went wrong with my demeanour and appearance?

I wore a suit and tie and spoke English well, but with a phoney English accent, which may have contributed to the adverse reaction.

Was I duped, or was it just bad luck? I stayed with the host, his Danish family, and friends for whatever reason. It would be an agonising experience from which I could not escape with dignity. The ordeal would convince me that I was a masochist.

My fellow countryman made fun of me throughout supper. My demeanour, in general, struck him as bourgeois.

It was indeed a show, albeit at my expense. Did Henry mistake me for someone else? His Danish wife––whose demeanour implied she was submissive––and their four children, two Danish men and three women, made up the audience.

Henry was a peculiar man whose offensive behaviour resulted from alcohol or drug use. He reminded me of a specific sort of Guyanese, precisely, male. When inebriated, show-offs would act as if it were their way of hurling insults at others (friends and adversaries), a type of retaliation for previous grievances.

Henry's demeanour shifted yet remained deceptive as he drank beer after beer. As I watched him, the image of a tragic hero emerged in my mind's eye.

Was alcohol the culprit or the man's character?

The following question kept *me* company to the end of Christmas Day: *why had I not, at once, excused myself from the musician's home?*

I did exit after Henry had fallen asleep. The mockery––the show––had ended. His sympathetic spouse apologised for her husband's behaviour. With an unnatural flair of piousness, I heard myself say, "I've forgiven your husband, father of your children, in the spirit of Christmas." I added, "Many lose themselves during this time of the year, the most festive of all seasons."

As I was leaving, I slighted the hippies who appeared earlier to have relished "the show," judging from their tittering.

Outside, winter air was colder but fresher than the atmosphere of London. My clothing needed airing out, for it had the scent of hash. It appeared like the snow's reflective properties had brought some welcome illumination to the night.

Safe in the confines of my hotel room, I attempted to make sense of Henry's uncouth manner. He had said, "I know your type." He had me down to be from a well-off family in Guyana––which was by no means the case. He had a sister who was one of Prime Minister Forbes Burnham's cabinet ministers. I assumed Henry had an axe to grind, and my persona may have awakened ghosts from his past. He had fired questions at me as if to test my general knowledge. I answered them as best I could, which he regarded as typical "bourgeois Guyanese." I remained rational and took all the insults and criticism he threw at me.

TO GET AWAY FROM COPENHAGEN, I departed early the following day to take a ferry to Malmö. The city itself wasn't the problem. I crossed my fingers and wished for better luck in the second-holiday phase.

I phoned a guy called Pete from the Copenhagen terminal, who sounded sober and cordial, which was a comfort. He promised to meet me at the ferry terminal in Malmö, Sweden. I had doubts about visiting those guys after my ordeal. But positive thinking took over and got the better of me.

Pete was a short guy who smiled and joked a lot. Like Adrian, he came from Grenada. I instantly took to him. By bus, we made our way to where he resided, a concrete tenement building. The apartment was spacious, and Pete shared it with three friends.

I eventually met a welcoming bunch of West Indians from Antigua, St. Lucia, and Saint Kitts. They made a livelihood by doing manufacturing labour, cleaning, or working as dishwashers in restaurants or bars.

They had plans to start a steel band group. There was, however, a need for more members, and they were considering hiring some Swedes interested in learning to play music on tuned petroleum drums. They intended to bring in Swedes to give the Caribbean band a more cosmopolitan flavour.

Their hopes were for Adrian, the doctor, to assist them with the necessary paperwork to submit to a local governing body.

I asked them whether they aimed to attract West Indians to Copenhagen. "No, man," said Pete. "'em boys have their own thin' going." I couldn't help mentioning that I had met Henry.

They burst out laughing in unison. Ralph, a St. Lucian, asked, "How is he?"

"His usual self," I said. "It was the first time we met."

"Dat man is a whole bundle of trouble when he takes a few drinks!"

"I know. I got a taste of it!" We all laughed.

The conversation shifted to other topics. We talked about their life in Sweden and for how long. They didn't have much to complain about Sweden.

"You find good and bad people everywhere," said Pete.

The others nodded.

I asked how they got on with the language. Reasonably okay, they said, adding that there were always comments about their poor pronunciation of some words and incorrect grammar. In England, the comments were similar; they stressed. I agreed.

The impression I got from them was that, at times, Swedes delivered critical comments in good faith.

We chatted and joked about things in general, in Caribbean style. We began listening to music, predominantly Jamaican Ska and Trinidadian Calypso. No Christmas Carols! Some Swedish and West Indian women and some American men appeared in the afternoon, and a seemingly spontaneous Boxing Day party began in full swing.

I danced with some women, but I didn't get anywhere. It did not matter, for I was in excellent spirits after my ordeal on Christmas Day, and almost everyone was smoking hash and marijuana.

I first tried it with two English guys years ago. I hung out in a Coffee Bar on Old Brompton Road, London. I don't remember experiencing anything "special" until Fred's get-together party when it got the better of me.

An American guy greeted me, "Hey, man! What's up? Take this; it will take you to Wonderland!" It was a purple heart pill. I thanked him and said I would take it later.

"No, man, now!" he said.

I made a face and pretended to pop it into my mouth. The American guy fell for the trick.

"That's the spirit, man!" he said. "Happy Holidays!" He wobbled off. He was a huge fellow with a high-pitched voice. I had him down to be a musician, but he was in Germany with the American Army.

Later I threw the pill into the southern breeze as I made my way to a backyard latrine. It reminded me of the ones in Georgetown for low-income families and rural areas of the country.

The next day I caught a nine o'clock morning train to Stockholm. A gang of rowdy youngsters rode in the carriages. One or two grown-ups appeared asleep while some elderly white people suffered in silence.

The youngsters weren't on their best behaviour, seeming oblivious to the concerns of adults. The mood was happy, though, even though I had trouble reading. I couldn't change carriages since it was too late.

My eyes now averted to the quick passing of the Swedish countryside, hoping to become sleepy – my thoughts on Guyana and its tropical landscape of perpetual green.

The Swedish countryside appeared and vanished in constant motion. There are vast areas of snowy fields and forests, farmland, tractors, and machinery operated by white figures at a distance. Part of the landscape consisted of isolated huts and several houses in small or large towns and rural villages. Apart from the architecture of dwellings and other structures, they may be identical to those in England.

The train arrived at Stockholm Central Station shortly after four o'clock in the afternoon. I made a few phone calls and eventually reached Ken, a Trinidadian who instructed me to take a train to Odenplan Underground Station. I had to wait an hour before Ken, and three others showed up in an old green Ford Escort. A Barbadian called George, a Grenadian named Nick, and a Guyanese called Monty. They were full of wit and tales on many topics. They were friendly people.

I inquired about the experience of living in Stockholm.

"Not like London," Ken said. He yearned for London.

"London, I like that city," Nick said. "I had a marvellous time there. I miss the clubs, but not the low wages." We all laughed.

"I missed London too," George said. "I go over once a year. But I prefer Stockholm to London for decent living quarters and working conditions."

"Sweden is better for students and finding an ordinary job," Monty said. "London is better if your ambition extends to higher things, like a career. There are no black bus or rail drivers in Sweden or taxi drivers."

I wanted to know why studying here was better.

"Well, for one thing, tuition is free, excluding books and living expenses."

I inquired how the average Swede differed from the average Englishman in terms of mentality.

"Not much difference," Ken said. "They both believe they are better than us. That's a notion shared by many white individuals, not only Swedes. I suppose the attitude is universal."

"He seems to equate your level of intelligence with how you speak Swedish," George said, laughing. We all laughed.

"Some make fun of how your Swedish sounds," Nick said.

"It's the same experience for foreign workers everywhere," George said. "We complain, and they complain."

"Discriminatory practices are difficult to discern," Monty said. "Many Swedes can come across as reticent or shy. Some look at us, but generally on the sly. Some avoid eye contact."

Later in the chat, I learned from George that most Swedes weren't outspoken or abusive as some English folks could be. The society was homogeneous, and most Swedes weren't used to seeing black people, which you noticed in the countryside – turning you into a novelty.

George worked in a home for the elderly. He spoke of patients and fellow personnel touching his hair and asking questions about his culture and customs. George wasn't offended and considered it normal. He once joked about being curious about white people as a child in Barbados.

I understood that in Stockholm, there were far fewer black folks: some musicians, a few students, some sailors, and some factory workers.

They spoke of white foreign factory workers: Finns, Italians, Greeks, Yugoslavians, Eastern Europeans, and perhaps to a lesser extent, Danes and Norwegians.

I asked the guys if Dr Adrian often visited Stockholm. They said he did and stayed in Solna with his girlfriend, Yvana. The men appeared to hold him in high regard. They regarded him as a down-to-earth guy.

I viewed these men as a group of calm individuals who did not appear "sensitive" to the biases of white people — unlike myself.

I stayed at (STF Vandrahem af Chapman) through Monty's recommendation, a ship converted into a hostel for mostly young tourists, like hitchhikers.

I went to the Golden Circle jazz club on Sveavägen and was surprised by Bill Evans' presence there. I went there with Monty, for the other guys weren't jazz fans, mostly calypso or soul.

Monty also took me to a New Year's Eve party in Gärdet held by an Eritrean art student with an unruly bushy hairdo. He was friendly and carried a warm smile. I met a Swedish girl, a post-graduate student of political science. Most of the folks there were students.

Vera later invited me to her place in the same building. She was a single mother with a five-year-old son, an attractive blonde, tall and slim, and blonde. It was a one-night stand for us.

I thought of Sweden and fantasised about living there, working, and studying. I shared such thoughts with Linnea in letters, still in Ghana, where she did voluntary work at a hospital clinic in a village. She wrote about the disadvantaged and the rich, two contrasting worlds.

I began to tell myself that the time had come to leave the mother country, alias my "Mecca." There were indeed joyous moments but too many unhappy ones. I hadn't fared well in *Inglan*. Nevertheless, in the few years I lived there, I gained knowledge and insight into human behaviour.

LINNEA WAS BACK FROM Ghana. She surprised me with the news that she could arrange for me to work for six months at a hospital that supplied accommodation. That would be the case if I genuinely contemplated working in Sweden. I would have to apply for a work visa at the Swedish Consulate in London. I informed her in an email that I wanted to spend a few months in Stockholm to see how things went.

After obtaining a work permit that took weeks, I gave in my notice to leave the job. My workmates treated me to a drink after work one Friday afternoon. I got a pen as a going-away present. My workmates joked, "You'll be back, Harry!" I laughed, hoping they were wrong.

Was it sensible to move to another country that spoke another language? I had to rely on my friend Linnea and a few new acquaintances to support me in an emergency. There isn't much certainty in life. I had learnt a thing or two since living in England. Surprisingly I was willing to take the chance.

I said goodbye to London in May to pursue dreams probably still propelled by a neurotic streak. The Scandinavian capital would be more open than London, a harsh city. I had underestimated what it meant to dwell in a big city – the chill that prevailed from its ambience and human souls. I would miss my new friends in Oxfordshire, the company of Caribbean friends at the Student Centre, Don and Leo, my GP, Mrs Mary Rogers, and the Lutheran priest-therapist.

TWO IDEAS BOLSTERED my confidence. One was Linnea's promise to get me a temporary job in a hospital. The other was that I arranged for a leave of absence from my London job. The venture was an opportunity to discover something new and that life was about taking risks. Living in fear of making mistakes was perhaps typical of many people, but what a terrible way to live! Better to try and fail than never to try at all -- in the words of a poet.

In the back of my mind was the hope of doing better in Sweden. I had no illusions that my situation would be straightforward. There was a new language to learn. I needed to keep my feet on the ground, judging cases as they unfolded and avoiding expecting too much at the onset. The situation appeared better than when I arrived in Britain. A menial job but one all the same, which was fine with me. I was determined to be resilient and headed for Sweden.

STOCKHOLM WASN'T AS big as London but bigger than Georgetown. The impression from the few West Indians during my brief visit seemed to contain some hope because it stayed with me during the early days and weeks. The generalisation that the average Swede was shy and reserved might be the case. I would be a stranger again in another country. In a few weeks, I discovered Swedes were no different from folks in other countries.

Some Swedes were part of a greaser subculture (working-class youth and older) popularly known as "ragggare." They wore black leader jackets and jeans, an Elvis Presley hairstyle, and held a beer can in one hand. The steering wheel of an American muscle car in the other, and roaring rock'n'roll music in the evening air.

Some people were unabashedly lovely, regardless of socioeconomic background. I found it easier to talk to Swedes in the street because they appeared more polite than Londoners.

My first few weeks in the Scandinavian city of Stockholm have been fantastic. Perhaps the smoothness was due to the Swedish character or a change in attitude that left my worries and neuroses in the Englishman's backyard.

I don't have a quarrel with the Swede in a historical sense, which was a good thing. My historical connection with the English people remained a source of discontent. I am the product of British colonialism.

I wasn't expecting my life to be without problems. The virus of racial hatred appeared wherever humans existed. I imagined the pattern of ethnic hostility is likely to be different in some ways and similar. There must be a sizable number of Swedes who feel superior to persons of colour.

For my part, it was so far an assumption, treading the slippery path of preconception. It would take a while for the experience to challenge my preconceived ideas, to shatter whatever illusions I treasured of this Nordic land.

Some of its inhabitants consider themselves to be Viking descendants. I believe that humankind is a product of social norms, practices, history, myths, perceptions, beliefs, and feelings of being different from other nationalities.

I wouldn't overstate the Swede, his distinction, because similar and dissimilar human traits govern him and me.

The Englishman, like the Guyanese, is imprisoned by his history, culture, social habits, and so on. I grew bored of British society's obsession with class and race.

5
STOCKHOLM

SWEDEN SHOULD BE DIFFERENT, and I'm betting on it. I was interested in seeing if my life would improve––a brighter future. I didn't want to lend significance to its homogenous culture, but I'm sure I'll gain a better grasp later.

With some people, their problems seemed to follow them everywhere like shadows. Leaving England appeared like a win and gave me a sense of satisfaction. If Sweden turned out to be worse than anticipated, my common sense would give me the strength to return to Guyana.

In due course, I hoped to get the ball rolling by finally starting higher education. I was free of the need to impress the Englishman, and I had no desire to impress Sweden's hosts and hostesses––a demand I considered absurd. I had grown weary of the obsession to become "somebody," which seemed to be the main reason for my restlessness. I planned to become a practising Christian and maybe follow in my mother's footsteps.

MY TIME IN SWEDEN PASSED quickly, and my situation there turned out to be better than I anticipated, which might have been due to the local atmosphere and my disposition. I began my work in the sterilisation department at the hospital, renting a room from the hospital. I was fortunate to obtain a job with no knowledge of the Swedish language. I could communicate in English, picking up a few Swedish words, phrases, and sentences.

Three evenings a week, I attended a "Swedish for Foreigners" course at TBV (a non-governmental institution for learning). Writing and grammar were easy-going; understanding verbal Swedish and speaking it was another matter.

The flow of the language became a challenge for me. A tall German guy at work, who was twice my age, had recommended I read children's books, for that was how he'd learned Swedish. I followed his advice, and such reading did help me to form simple and compound sentences.

Evening lessons in grammar, syntax, and phonetics remained crucial. I met a kind Pole in the Swedish Course for Beginners, who occasionally helped me. Richard, a newbie, planned to pursue his doctorate in Sweden. He studied French, German, and Russian at the university level in Poland.

If there were such a thing as an average citizen of any country, I would describe the average Swede as self-effacing, reserved, and laconic. In public places, the Swede carries an unsmiling face. If the Swede does see you or look you in the eye, he may stare or risk a glimpse before shifting his gaze. The Swede does not show off, unlike many Guyanese. I heard someone saying that Swedes shy away from conflicts where they rarely show anger.

There were people like that in every country. I was used to looking at people in passing, but now I do it the Swedish way, with my eyes turned away, so I don't get annoyed by how some people look at me.

My voice rises when I become angry. I found myself admiring another Swedish way by not allowing my anger to get into the form of whatever I intended to say. Over the years, I noticed my verbal aggression had inevitably overshadowed whatever I wanted to convey. My manner was typical of Guyanese.

Once you get to know the Swede, you will likely have a trusted friend – which is more than I can say about most English people I have met in London.

Romantic relationships were now on the back burner, for they had a way of distracting me from matters of importance. I was preoccupied with learning Swedish as quickly as possible and pursuing higher education. I wanted a break from the sexual politics of love: disappointments and the inevitable misunderstandings between two incompatible souls.

Many attractive women appeared proportionally more than English women in London in Stockholm. But my habit of eyeing women with pretty faces and figures in the streets continued, although discreetly. I imagined their personalities at times. Perhaps my fascination with the feminine body was a symptom of my prolonged adolescence. I have been in the company of Swedish men who weren't overly carried away by the sight of feminine beauty.

Sometimes I was embarrassed by my manner. I had to harness my sexual passions, regarding myself as weak to lustful desires. The idea of celibacy came to me to quell the intense longing that drove me. I decided to test abstinence to find out how important sex was in my life. I read somewhere that it was less important than the need for sleep or food.

I later allowed myself to have a couple of dates without needing intimacy, which was enjoyable. Stockholm's picturesque locations were a wonderful distraction.

I OCCASIONALLY WENT to the movies on Saturdays or Sundays, shopped or visited bookshops in Stockholm City or dropped by Kungsträgården (the national park) to see if a buddy was around. I occasionally encountered George, Ken, and Nick at the national park, but Monty was rarely there. I would stroll along a river at Djursgården, within walking distance of the shopping area, but I sometimes used the tram.

I bought a Sony camera, and my interest in "picture-taking" became a hobby. The old town (Gamla Stan) offered scenery, restaurants, and cafés, and it had cobblestone streets and buildings yellow and brown. The frescoes from the Middle Ages, beautiful churches, and a museum; Bergius Botanic Garden and Park, the Royal Dramatic Theatre, Skansen Open-Air Museum, and Gröna Lund, an amusement park.

I learned that Stockholm was situated on 14 islands, and its centre stood on water. The South of the town was beautiful. It offered a vibrancy reminiscent of a few Greater London boroughs, with many cafes and restaurants, pubs, antique shops, art shops, and boutiques.

At the time, I had little to complain about my life in Sweden. The positives outweighed the negatives. Like every European society, I assumed racial prejudice and discrimination existed on structural and personal levels. Later I encountered racial prejudice because of being denied access to one or more clubs, where membership was a pretext.

The discriminatory behaviour wasn't as severe as I had encountered in London. In Stockholm, there were fewer black people: some were musicians, seamen, university students, and factory workers. I met non-Swedes, mostly Finns, some Italians, Greeks, Danes, and Norwegians – all with preconceived notions of black folk.

I noticed that the Swedes I met had a better geographical knowledge of other countries. For example, they knew where Guyana was. It was the opposite in Britain. It had less to do with their education level and more with a colonialist mentality or ignorance. *Was Guyana part of Jamaica?*

Another difference in comparing the Swede and the Englishman was that the Englishman was more outspoken about his dislike of other races.

What a broad statement! I know. Of course, I'm not a social scientist but a layperson with the prerogative to get things wrong.

Having learned my lesson in London, I wasn't expecting Sweden to be a "paradise on Earth." I fared well in the early months. I had no desire to return to England or Guyana, and I no longer wished to live in the USA.

6

STOCKHOLM

AFTER A YEAR, MY HOSPITAL work continued, and I sought a transfer to the patient transport area and was successful. I started after a one-week vacation in London, where I met old friends at the Student Centre. They were curious about my impressions of Sweden, and I was glad to pass them on because there was a certain admiration attached to leaving England for Europe. I liked the idea of playing a tourist who acquired status in the motherland. My feelings of displeasure, complaints, and bitterness toward England had disappeared. I missed the English language, my mother tongue, although it would interfere with my efforts to communicate in Swedish.

The situation caused me to reflect on the difficulty some Indian migrants encountered in Britain. Then, via my own experience, I realised the severity of their linguistic challenges.

Being away from England has provided me with some insight.

I LIKED THE CHANCE to chat as I moved patients in beds or wheelchairs from wards to clinics with a group of porters. I would interact with hospital staff from the wards and clinics.

Many of the porters were young men who had recently graduated from high school and were serving a six-month stint before doing military service. A tiny proportion of middle-aged men and women may have worked in patient transportation.

During breaks, I would chat with my workmates in English. Some, for whatever reason, were difficult to approach and appeared uninterested. There were at least two individuals who admitted to being xenophobic. Their harsh comments aimed at blacks and Middle Easterners. I managed to keep my irrational feelings in check.

The few years I spent in England helped, although I occasionally lost my cool and became verbally emotional. I wasn't the only one who wasn't Swedish in the group. There was a Palestinian, a Senegalese, two Yugoslavians, a Finn, two Danes, and a Norwegian among them. They were all guys.

The Norwegian was easy to talk to; he had a sense of humour, but occasionally a racial joke about Africans would come from him. As someone in London once remarked, I had trouble ignoring some racist remarks not to appear oversensitive. One Dane was okay; he liked talking to me about American and British literature, while another was moody and not much for idle talk.

The Finnish man of fifty years of age wasn't optimistic about my race. He had once told me that he was proud that Finland wasn't allowing too many black people to live there. I remember asking him why he left Finland. But the Finn only smiled as if my question didn't make sense. He could have considered it his privilege as a Nordic citizen.

Most Yugoslavians were easy to get on with; they talked and joked with me in Swedish. They even taught me a few words in Serbian. They were not overjoyed to live in Sweden. It was mainly for economic reasons because they loved their country and visited it once a year. One intended to return only for a holiday. I remember one named Slobodan, who changed his Mercedes car yearly.

I developed an interest in vehicles, including sports cars. I needed the means to buy a car and obtain a driving license.

7

STOCKHOLM

SOME AFTERNOONS AFTER work, I went into town. I usually dropped by a café in ABF-*huset* where a few Afro-Americans and fellow West Indians were hanging out. I'd look for friendly blacks because some black people had an attitude towards black strangers and treated them as *invisible*. I introduced myself, but it was to no avail. I considered they were in no hurry to get to know me and shared a similar attitude to some Swedes. Later, I experienced some Americans as vain as some West Indians. Afro-Americans were often suspicious of possible CIA informers in their midst. I even recalled Swedish (Maoists) students who warned me about such infiltration. My accent in Swedish made me sound American and not British.

One afternoon I witnessed an argument between two of my fellow citizens at that cafe. They weren't my friends at the time. Both had ignored me for some time. Martin and Stanley accused each other of having an affair with a woman.

At length, a fistfight erupted. I supposed that was common for some men in any country because I knew it was the same in Guyana.

I preferred a café in *Kungsträdgården* to that café near ABF-*huset*. I would spend most of my time there before attending Swedish classes at TBV. Several of the faces I knew were often there. They and I became friends. Robert took some technical studies, and John was a musician, and both were from Trinidad.

Gerry was Guyanese and worked in some factory or other. He had resided in London since he was 10 or 12, and we would hang out now and then in discos. Later, Gerry became a Jehovah's Witness, making trips to some Eastern European countries. I lost contact with him.

Another Guyanese friend was Steve, who did mental health work. I enjoyed talking to him. He was psychologically minded and bookish like me. We both had an interest in psychology and human behaviour. He encouraged me to become a mental health worker, but I wasn't keen on working with the mentally ill at the time.

Richard worked as a car mechanic, had served in the British Army, and came from one of the Caribbean islands. Reggie was a singer who did not mix with blacks, whom he considered under his social status and preferred the society of Swedes. He boasted about knowing persons of importance in London with whom he was on friendly terms. There was Jimmy, the jazz ballet dancer and streetwise. Roy and Dave were musicians and salesmen, selling art replicas from house to house in various Swedish towns.

MY WORK IN THE HOSPITAL offered nothing more than occasional conflicts with work colleagues and unfair distribution of work. Some days the situation was fair. Sometimes it was the other way around. I knew I had more work than some colleagues and a job that no one liked.

This work included collecting sacks used as garbage containers when the weather was windy or wet, with heavy rain or snowfall. The four infection clinics were Oncenext to the main hospital. I transported clean beds from the bed section to some wards in elevators or patients in beds through a long corridor to psychiatric or geriatric wards.

The foreman was an active member of the workers' union, and he favoured some Swedish porters more than other porters from other countries.

Sometimes I protested, but it didn't help. So I accepted the unfair situation and told myself I'd look for something better once I knew Swedish well enough. I also had a book that I could read on my breaks. It was a pleasant distraction that helped me forget about the problems at work.

The foreman once requested that I carry a corpse to the morgue, but I lied and said it was against my religion. I got that excuse from a Palestinian guy exempted from such a task. There was, however, no escaping the assignment; after a few times, it became part of my job.

Once a week, I would go to the emergency clinic's cold storage to get the dead body of a person. Or at any time during the day from the wards. I recall a male corpse with red, purple, and blue markings on his neck and upper chest. Someone said that he might have suffered a heart attack or accident.

When I arrived at the morgue, I'd slide the body onto a steel table and place a wooden block at the nape of its neck. A body fetched from the wards was sometimes warm, which came from the wards. The worst was transporting an infant corpse in a white wooden box to the morgue.

Occasionally my duties covered lunch or dinner deliveries to various wards in sizeable wagons pulled by a small three-wheeled truck.

8

STOCKHOLM

PERRY WAS A MIXTURE of Portuguese and African and overweighed. He hailed from a tiny Caribbean Island and did economics at Stockholm University. He was full of himself, condescending to others, face to face and behind their backs. I played badminton with him and lost most of the time, and when I won, Perry said it was luck. I had him down to have an inferiority complex that prompted his compulsive need to notice others' flaws. The women he dated were of a "higher class" than those his friends and I dated. I had mixed feelings about him. Sometimes I liked to visit him. Other times, when his nasty attitude emerged, I was petrified.

Murphy was a Guyanese and a language student at Stockholm University. He always carried his student card in a transparent shirt pocket to impress women.

Chester hailed from Jamaica and dressed smartly, bearing semblance to an English Earl or Lord.

Then there was Woodley. He hailed from the Caribbean and was secretive about his country of origin. His friends called him "Woodley the Conqueror," for he often pursued "a new woman" as if from compulsion. He was unconcerned with insults from ladies he was interested in and was often successful in his romantic endeavours. Woodley kept count of the women bedded since leaving his country for England. He spent a few years there before coming to Sweden.

One week at the Ambassador nightclub, Woodley picked up seven women—one each night. He was not someone to lie about such a thing. I saw him many a time during his pursuits. He was a top-class dancer: his tall, slim body moved effortlessly. Woodley knew he wasn't handsome, but good-looking features didn't always do the trick. He relied on charisma, bravery, and a silver tongue that had served Woodley well. He had a Barry White voice.

Woodley once boasted to us, a clique of friends, that he had pretended to be an economic student in London to impress au pair girls from various European countries.

In Sweden, he dropped that student's act, he said. Woodley worked at the Post Office in the city, delivering packages. In his pursuit of a woman, Woodley often strayed from the truth. He would often describe himself as a musician.

Getting to know Woodley, I discovered he had no interest in dating women more than a couple of times. He was generous in introducing his friends to the ladies he had previously dated. His chief objective seemed to attain fast love or, in his words, "sweet love."

I would lose contact with Woodley, for he emigrated to the Big Apple. Woodley wasn't one for writing letters. He had sent me a card or two about his "good times" and "sweet love," but then no news came from him. Rumour had it that he had met some wealthy woman from Los Angeles. Another rumour claimed that a jealous woman shot him. Whatever I would think of him and others like him. He did not fit a gigolo description because his seduction was without a financial price tag. He remained a mysterious fellow.

9

STOCKHOLM

MY JOB WAS GETTING dull, but I decided to bear the frustration. I wanted to understand how long I'd manage without becoming self-destructive, like giving up my job and returning to London. My former boss in London, Mr Mc Donald, said my return would be welcome. I had another alternative: to return to Guyana. But could it still be a safe zone for me?

On my agenda was the desire to embark on higher learning. I had to prove to my father and a few people at the Student Centre in London that I wasn't a simpleton.

An individual who frequented the Student Centre came to mind: Jacques hailed from Martinique or Guadeloupe. One day, he noticed me reading Jean-Paul Sartre's *La Nausée* in English. He maliciously remarked that I would not understand the book, giggling as he went his way. I thought of the absurdity of the man, of medium height, with a bearded face that often carried a silly smile and delusions of grandeur. We have never had a dispute before.

I rather liked the guy. I remember him relating anecdotes and receiving laughter from listeners. He knew British novelist Doris Lessing who lived around the corner from the West Indian Students' Centre, 1 Collingham Gardens, Earls Court, London, UK.

Jacques spoke of amusing details of well-known folks in Paris, primarily the Caribbean diaspora. He was an aspiring writer or might have published a book. Jacques worked in an office, wore a suit, sported a bow tie and a pipe, and carried a briefcase. I did not know what he did for a living. Sometimes, negative remarks from others can inspire me.

IN THE AUTUMN, I ENROLLED at Stockholm University and chose to read English and Education. I'd study those subjects part-time. I now had the confidence to tackle and manage Swedish in writing and speech and had a competent knowledge of the spoken language.

My vocabulary had increased, but I still had much left concerning vocabulary, grammar, and pronunciation. I got used to Swedes correcting my Swedish or even, at times, making fun of my accent––and why not? Some English folks did the same, though mainly for pleasure. The idea humiliated me that my Caribbean English accent got trampled.

I had the idea that my Swedish would expand through becoming a student in subjects that I liked. It turned out to be the case. After work, I became busy, attending lectures and seminars twice a week. I taught "Conversational English" to senior citizens at ABF twice a week in the evenings. Still, I had to reduce it to my tight weekly schedule once a week.

I would go into town to socialise with friends at Tudor Arms for a couple of hours on Fridays or Saturdays. It was an English pub, where I met two English guys, Jim and John, street musicians. They were okay, guys.

I noticed English blokes were different in Sweden, and I'm not sure why. Of course, they had views about the Swedes––negative remarks most non-Swedes aired.

At the pub, I met one or two Englishmen from Stockholm's British Embassy or business community. My tutors were both English and Swedish at the university in the English faculty.

I OBTAINED A VACANT post at the hospital in the lining storage section, delivering laundry in two one-meter wagons to the wards and clinics. Two of us did the job, including collecting dirty laundry later fetched by a trunk to a laundry factory in *Rimbo,* roughly 43 km away. Bertil, one of my workmates, was a Swede from *Piteå* in *Norrbotten* and of my age or older. He was a man of few words and shy, but I got along with him well. He knew a bit of English and helped me with Swedish by correcting my mispronunciation. I was grateful to him, Bertil. With that work, I carried out my duties quickly. I found time to read the material or a book from my university courses.

I BEGAN TO ATTEND THE black-owned disco Busby's Joint. After months of celibacy, I regarded it as an act of spiritual cleansing. At the disco were strange characters of both sexes, black and white. The atmosphere was multicultural, and the presence there gave me a feeling of happiness and joy. It was almost like an integrated environment in London. Most of the women appeared confident. The white woman danced like black women; a swaying of shoulders, hips, and buttocks propelled a movement that enchanted the minds of men. Many black men there were strangers to me: African men and women and men from the Caribbean and America. The music was a mixture of American soul and African.

After regular visits to Busby's Joint, the crowd became regulars. The women turned out to be primarily exhibitionists, teasers who seemed ready to make fun of unfamiliar faces. The men looked like ego-trippers and criminal types. I continued to visit there, primarily to rendezvous with friends and not show interest in befriending any of the women. Occasionally, I became interested in an unfamiliar female face. Some Caribbean men took pride in meeting a woman who was a newcomer to the disco. Dating a regular woman at Busby's Joint was like asking for trouble. I had witnessed a few angry arguments that led to fights between men and women. A few of the people I knew avoided the disco.

Woodley avoided Busby's Joint, having set foot there once. Reggie, the singer, had a similar attitude towards the place. Richard, the car mechanic, avoided the Joint and only attended dance halls and clubs with only a handful of black faces.

Entering some clubs wasn't a straightforward matter. I visited such a club with Woodley once or twice; the Swedish men were on firm ground there, and black men appeared to be weak competitors. Some Swedish men would even make a play at whichever Swedish woman showed an interest in a dark-skinned male. Sometimes they would succeed; I did experience losing a lovely woman to a Swedish man. I wasn't offended, for he was on home territory, where I might have been second best or less.

I experienced something similar while dating one of the few Caribbean women in Stockholm. She ditched me for a Swede. "All in love is fair" is a song by Stevie Wonder.

IN LONDON, I HAD INITIALLY expected to meet English folks who treated me with respect. But in time, I gave up and settled for a couple of trusted English folks with whom to socialise. They were not concerned about the colour of my skin or nationality or anything like that.

I had a few Swedish friends who were decent folks: my skin colour wasn't a stumbling block to friendship. I met Emil and Allan at a tennis club.

I met a few Swedish friends when I became a student. Thomas was one of them, and he and I would play tennis whenever we had the time.

I met Dr Nils Jansson, who worked at the hospital where I worked. Nils was a compassionate Swede, he wanted to go to Africa to work, but marriage and family had ended his dream. He invited me once a month for dinner, and we had discussions about Africa and the Caribbean. Dr Nils Jansson and I agreed on most matters. He encouraged me to study to become a psychologist, impressed with my layperson knowledge.

I wasn't interested in becoming a psychologist. I might've disappointed him. Our contact continued but was not as frequent as before. He still invited me to dinner from time to time with his wife and three children and a few of his friends who were also doctors.

Looking back, I met a few Swedes, men and women, who regarded me in a favourable light. They gave me advice, which I appreciated. I felt that their dreams for my future didn't fit well with mine. I remember meeting a Jewish doctor who suggested I study to become a psychotherapist; she admired my experiences and assessments of people and life. I wasn't interested.

I wondered why I had ignored sound advice from people who wanted me to shine. The Swedes I hung out with were mainly an ambitious lot. I remember feeling pressured by their desire for me to rise above my present level. I felt unsure of my ability.

I badly lacked self-confidence. I couldn't understand why; it would remain a part of me like my shadow.

10

STOCKHOLM

I CONTINUED TO PHONE my mother once a month. Grandpa Adam had passed away a few months before; my parents were still a couple. My mum had problems with her back and mild rheumatism. My father had suffered a stroke that left him frail. He still smoked, but his drinking habit was gone. Peace and goodwill were between my father and me, conducted through letters.

My mother had made it possible; she had encouraged the conciliation. My dad's handwriting was difficult to read because of the stroke. So, my mother had taken to writing his letters while he dictated them. My mum firmly believed my dad, and I would benefit from the conciliation.

She also thought that making peace between father and son was active in the Christian tradition and serving my father and me well in the eyes of God. She reminded me that atonement was essential for a troubled soul and that sometimes we only get a chance in such matters.

For the love of my mother, I went through with it. My fear of God's wrath, eternal damnation, fire, and brimstone may have contributed to this.

Through the letters, I learned of my father's regrets and that he would've been lenient if given a second chance. I wrote of my "love and affection" for him and regretted my unruly behaviour. While writing to him, I'd struggle to hold back tears of sadness and sorrow that resided in the chambers of my soul.

I still suffered from having lost out on a loving father-and-son relationship. I would later realise that forgiving wasn't that simple. I wasn't a Jesus figure.

I wrote to him about my life, taking responsibility, and the wisdom I got from him, but I wasn't in the right mind to benefit from it. I wrote about my menial work and my university studies.

Then I got word from Sandra that our mum had colon cancer.

The news shocked the hell out of me. I immediately applied for a two-week vacation to visit my parents in Guyana. After some fuss from my boss, I was granted the time off, and after a flight to London and Trinidad, I finally reached Guyana.

From the airport, it took an hour or more by car to get to my parents. The scenery appeared different after being away from Guyana––the roads seemed narrow, the streets smaller, and the houses, including my parents, appeared worse. However, that might not have been the case, for my memory had played a trick on me.

My parents were overjoyed to see me, especially my mum. I was filled with joyful tears and affected by her state of health. She had had a quick operation and appeared pale. My mother had lost her appetite; her doctor had recommended sweet beverages as a stimulant for the low desire To take any job to eat, but she still struggled. She was going to die, and her family and sisters knew it was only a matter of time.

I was in denial. I prayed and prayed and prayed for my mother to recover.

My mum wasn't afraid to die, she told me. She spoke of going to heaven where her dad, Grandpa Adam, was, and her mother. She said she had several dreams of entering the Pearly Gates. I did not want her to die, not then, not ever!

I couldn't envision my life without my mum, the only person I could love and trust. I tried to be rational; I didn't wish to add to her suffering and pain. I was conscious of my selfishness. I visited my aunts, but one of them, Macy, the youngest, had moved to Brooklyn, New York, where she worked as a nurse. Angelica and Eunice were considering moving to Toronto, Canada. It was nice seeing them and chatting.

My two aunts had written about Grandpa Adam's beautiful funeral: had got: it was "a pleasing turnout," a several-car procession, and many flowers from former workmates, friends, and neighbours. At the wake gathering, several men and women came. The men recounted pleasurable memories, amusing Grandpa Adam; the men played dominoes and drank to his soul.

I made a few visits to friends. Some I found, and others had gone abroad to study or the better their future. A few young men in my neighbourhood had died through natural causes or violence. One of the girls I liked but never got anywhere with had four kids; another had lost her life from an illegal abortion.

I didn't get to meet Sandra. She was in Canada, studying Economics in Montreal and had visited Guyana earlier in the spring.

MY MOTHER PASSED AWAY in her sleep one month after my visit. Sandra rang me at 2 a.m. Swedish time, on a Wednesday morning. The news of my mother's death sent me into shock. I felt a part of me had died. I cried, had called in sick at work, owing to immense grief. Monday, I returned to work.

For weeks, I mourned the loss of my mum. I read and re-read her letters I had kept in a shoebox, missing out on a couple of lectures and seminars at the university. I had given friends a rest. I took long walks in solitude, remembering her and our talks after my father temporarily kicked me out of the house. There was no grave to visit, only photos and her memory.

When she died, the reality became excruciatingly painful. I wished to die at the time, but there was no chance of it happening, not by my own hands. My mother's wish was for me to have a happy life. I had told her that I would be loyal to her desires.

I had not attended my mother's funeral. She and I had settled during my visit to Guyana. It meant more to her and me to meet for the last time. It had been vital to know; that there was no guilty conscience for not being at her funeral. Of her four children, only Sandra attended the funeral. Sandra had expressed her disappointment in me not attending. I don't believe she had forgiven me.

A couple of weeks later, I received a letter from Aunt Angelica. It came out of the blue, for I had not heard from her in a while. So, I imagined it to be the news of my mum's funeral. Her letter contained three photographs of the funeral. One photo was from the funeral service. Another picture presented a view of my mum in the casket, dressed in lily white, and her face was still beautiful. Even in slumber everlasting, my mother appeared as if she was merely asleep. The third photo showed the casket in her spot in the cemetery. Then there was the letter.

DEAR HARRY,

I hope this letter finds you in good health. Understandably the loss of your mommy has taken a toll on you, but you are not alone. The Good Lord is with you. We all are mourning her absence from this life. Your mommy, the loving soul she was, is now in safe hands. She will be greatly missed. You have always been special to her, and your aunties love you too. Your mommy had asked me to pass on a letter she wrote to you:

Your Loving Auntie Angelica

DEAR HARRY,

I've something to tell you that I had kept from you for so long because I believed it would not have served you well to know, and

it would likely have made matters worse between you and your dad. It will shock, but your dad and aunts have supported my decision. I asked the Lord for forgiveness, and now I ask you for your forgiveness and understanding: Your dad, Samuel Holmes, is not your "real dad," but he is by far a better person than your real father, who had turned his back on me and you. Your biological father declared his love for me and made promises he had not kept when I told him I was with his child. Your real dad had planned to study medicine in England, which was right, and so he went through with his plan, which was his promise to his father. He promised to write but never did, not once! Your stepfather had always been fond of me. Somehow, he learned about my broken heart and shame, and Mr Holmes had always wanted to marry me. Your stepdad loves you, Harry, although his foolish pride kicks in. I hope you will forgive me. God bless you and will always guide us against Satan if we don't lose faith and follow the devil's way. I remain your dear Mom, who always loved you and will visit you, with the Lord's Will, in your dreams, the same way your grandmother did to all her children.

Your affectionate mum,
Thelma Holmes

I REMEMBER THE SHOCK from the letter and the mixed sentiments I felt after reading it twice and thrice. My mum failed me by not letting me know earlier. It might have clarified things and helped me understand my relation to Samuel Holmes, which had always puzzled me. Why couldn't my mother find a way, with God's help, to tell me? After I became older enough to understand her ordeal and shame instead of hiding in a crib of secrecy.

I was angry, grieved, and bewildered: Such a well-kept secret for my benefit, not even a whisper, a sign, from loving Grandpa Adam's lips. Perhaps I was penalised for the sins of my bona fide father. This spineless creature set sail to become a medical doctor. To some degree, I blamed myself for the punishment I received from my stepfather. The hate in his eyes was the sign I had noticed but failed to construe.

I recall flinging the letter and envelope into the air, perplexed and enraged. It crashed against a wall in my room and then fell flat, probably depleted of force or gravitational pull.

The photographs had taken off in flight, lost momentum and landed in different spots.

I hated my mum and sisters, Grandpa Adam, stepbrother, stepsister, Sandra, and stepfather. In my little lodging, I believed they all were to blame for such a sinful act - a collective sin.

In fantasy and borrowing a page from the chronicle of monstrous deeds committed by Comrade Stalin, I ordered their execution by firing squad.

Then I broke down and cried tears of self-pity and fell asleep, my pillow saturated with tears and mucus and my body in a foetal position.

I woke up in the middle of the night and went under the bed covers because I shivered in the cold room.

In the morning, I decided to go to work to punish myself. I misbehaved.

I conducted a series of angry outbursts with workmates, visited my boss, and swore about my lousy job before I broke down, weeping with convulsive gasps.

My boss sat in his office, staring at my intrusion as if in mental paralysis.

Then I stopped and pulled myself together. I related my tragic situation, and my boss's response appeared sympathetic. I remember his persona, a man of few words who rarely smiled.

In the end, he instructed me to visit the personnel doctor, where I received one week's sick leave.

Three months later, my stepfather passed away in a nursing home for the elderly. I shed some tears, but that was all. I threw no tantrum or sorrow.

Only Sandra and Faye attended my dad's funeral.

11

STOCKHOLM

ONE FRIDAY AT BUSBY'S Joint, I got into a dispute with an American deserter. I rarely saw him alone: he always had two girls at his side. For whatever reason, I was invisible to him. My Caribbean friends received similar treatment. I was chatting with Anastasia, whom I had previously dated. She wasn't a regular at Busby's Joint. We were dancing when the Afro-American guy, Jack, approached Anastasia. Jack said something to her, seized her left arm, and led her away. I was astonished, not knowing what to think or do. I heard myself say, "Hey, what's that about?" With the eyes of a wildcat, the Afro-American came at me, giving me a head-butt. He roared, "Mind your own business!" He released his grip.

The head-butt was exceedingly painful, for my head felt as if I had gone into a stonewall.

The American turned and walked off; I cannot recall seeing Anastasia, for it was as if she had disappeared. My friends, cowards like me, stood there like spectators. They certainly weren't like some friends I had during my primary school days.

Later I would reflect on the incident. Anastasia was his ex-girlfriend, or was she and Jack in "business" together? I had never seen her in his company, or perhaps I had but didn't remember. Anastasia never once mentioned him.

Woodley informed me that Jack, the American, was involved in a few illegal ventures. "Maybe your friend Anastasia was part of his racketeering." I was shocked. I hadn't even thought that might be the case.

She had told me about her three brothers and one sister in Russia: they studied music, art, engineering, and architecture. Anastasia had come to Sweden because she wanted to go to America – by falling in love with an American soldier who would marry her and take her to the United States of America. Was that true? I now ask myself.

Woodley said he didn't fall for Anastasia's story. I bought her story.

Then one Saturday, on my way to a nine o'clock movie, I noticed Anastasia in a bar on *Kungsgatan*. She was with a white guy twice her age, someone from a seemingly higher social status, judging from his appearance.

For days, I blame myself for being gullible, not sensing her "game," despite my suspicious nature.

What did Anastasia want from me? The reason remained a riddle.

I gave up the Busby's Joint, regarding the women there as ladies of the night, wild and kinky, or God knows what! The dodgy crowd for my liking. My dad was right: mind the company you keep. The company you keep defines you say, he would say. I continued to drop by cafes and pubs that West Indians frequented, and I would choose to have only a few close friends.

12

STOCKHOLM

I WROTE TO SANDRA ABOUT the secret, which surprised her too. I chose not to mention the unpleasant encounter at Busby's Joint. More important things: to inform her about my job, studies, and attaining peace of mind. I wrote to Thomas, and Faye believed the decision made by mum and dad was right. They knew little about their true mother – who died while they were six or seven.

I hope to visit Sandra in Montreal, my aunt Macy in Brooklyn, Faye in Baltimore, and Thomas in Washington, DC.

I wrote to a few friends in Canada: Benny, Luke, and Winston. According to their letters, they were still the same in humour and manner. I lost contact with friends who went to America. I learned that Robby had gone to Vietnam and never was seen again until, one day, an acquaintance spotted him in ragged clothes in the street, with an unkempt beard and bushy hair. Robby had gone to the dogs. Sadly. My heart ached for his tragedy.

I have had fleeting thoughts of becoming a Mormon, rescuing young folks with lost hope for the future. My Caribbean friends jokingly told me, "You're one crazy man!"

I considered myself an eccentric figure, and I would smile at the thought. I haven't changed, but I have learned things from reading and experiencing, which is no different for most people. I'm still learning and struggling to listen more and do less talking.

AFTER THE DEATH OF my mother and stepfather, I sought some solitude in a church with memories of them. My love for her had survived the storm of my wrath. That first love in my life affected the love that I sought from other women. Something similar for D. H. Lawrence, I read.

A mother's love was unselfish and unconditional, the kind of love any man couldn't expect from any other woman. I might die a bachelor with no children to call my own. Should I fall short of finding love, I would peaceably resign to such a fate.

Recently I befriended a single Caribbean mother of three kids. She worked in the canteen at the hospital. If a love relationship develops between us, I wouldn't say no to a stepfather's role. Happiness had a way of showing up in places I had least expected.

I never became a Mormon. A fleeting desire. I read a magazine edition of their "brand" of religion but wasn't motivated enough. I was never good at becoming a group member or being part of anything. I'm no longer attending church. Though I haven't done that for years, I consider myself a Christian.

The problem was trust: I couldn't trust most church members; I regarded many as hypocrites. The church wasn't the only way to worship God. I settled for reading the Bible my mum sent me years ago. I'd read it when my mood was low. Music would continue to serve me well when the blues appeared––music: my second religion.

AT THE CULTURE HOUSE (*Kulturhuset*), I had brief discussions with black and white American deserters about current political and social issues related to American domestic issues and the Vietnam War. The suspicion of CIA informers in their company was of no concern to me; I wasn't the least bothered about who was or wasn't an informer.

I once heard from a Caribbean friend that I was a CIA informer. He learned of it in his attempt to make a move on a Swedish socialist feminist at Café Ricardo. She had asked him if he knew me. He said he did, and her interest in him faded.

I remember he and I laughed at the ridiculous idea of being an informer. I might have had a conversation with her, but one that escaped memory. Such were the times in some circles in Stockholm during the era of Make Love, Not War.

I attended a concert to raise money for a local Black Cultural Centre. A Ghanaian man, Badou and a black South African woman Joyce were founders of the Black Cultural Centre in *St. Eriksplan*. I visited there several times to play table tennis and watch others play cards. There was a plan to start a theatre group, and some fellow named Moby, an aspiring playwright and my countryman, had offered to write a play depicting the disharmony in the Black Diaspora in Stockholm. There might have been other activities which I missed.

I once ran into a few other Americans who seldom hung out in the city. One was married and had published a book. He described himself as a Marxist and later became a radio broadcaster in Albania.

I knew Sherman Adams, a vast Afro-American, once a boxer back home. He became a journalist and writer during his exile in Sweden. Sherman wrote articles about the problems and hardships that black Americans endured; wrote an autobiography in Swedish, which might've been translated.

I met an Italian American who went by the name of Mario at Stockholm University in the English department. He was a deserter, having spent some time in Spain working as a guard in a brothel before arriving in Stockholm.

I knew Karl La Corbiniere, a journalist with roots in a French Caribbean Island. He was a pleasant and knowledgeable guy. Herbert was the tall, red-skinned American who worked in a hospital lab.

"Mad Dog" (Willy) was an aggressive individual and deserter, often in a fight and always when he was drunk. He hated West Indians and Africans.

I met a white American who came to Sweden to avoid the draft (which ended in 1973) who was a college guy. We hung out, lunching on rice, sardines, brown bread, and peanut butter. We discussed Colin Wilson's book, The Outsider, and I remember feeling like an outsider, a marginal man. The book offered me examples of outsiders in literary works of fiction.

I reflected on arrogant folks from the Caribbean and Afro-Americans, for they were many in the Black Diaspora in Stockholm. Was it related to the fact that the world was white and that conceitedness (like the narcissist's false self, perhaps) was a booster of their self-esteem and well-being? Maybe it was a trait we all shared.

Did I meet *bad apple*s in Stockholm? I asked myself. There were *rotten apples* in Stockholm, but there wasn't any danger of me following the wrong company again, as it had been in London. Some Caribbean, African, and Afro-American folks did some illegal trade or another and got deported.

In general, Afro-Americans had their troubles. It couldn't have been fun becoming a deserter and spending the rest of one's existence in exile. But this was not to be, for President Carter granted a pardon for American deserters.

13

STOCKHOLM

AT THE UNIVERSITY OF Stockholm, my exams went well without re-sittings. I contemplated taking a leave of absence for one year to complete the BA degree earlier. Now that my stepfather was no longer alive, I had to prove I could obtain a university degree. After finishing, I would no longer worry about what kind of work I did. I became less concerned about work status, unlike in England. Swedes generally seemed less concerned about social class.

But I might have got it wrong. At least, that remained my impression. Of course, I had encountered snobbish individuals – from the Left and the Right on the political spectrum. To my mind, it wasn't how it was in England.

However, reality forced my hand, or was it instead of a change of mind? I had decided to apply for a two-year course at the secondary school level for mental health workers, providing me with 75% of my regular salary. On the other hand, a university degree would've pleased my ego while failing to give me a chance to attain a better job. Philosophy, or English at the PhD level, might have been better for obtaining employment. At least, that was what I gathered from a few fellow students in both faculties.

The situation changed in Sweden when a university's first degree provided you with the chance to receive training for some clerical work or other. Perhaps Dr Nils Jansson had been right to suggest that I study to become a psychologist, a 5-year course (master's degree). I went through the syllabus and got put off by its lengthy program, a full-time study.

Psychotherapy appealed more to me. A qualified psychologist needs further training to become a skilled psychotherapist. However, the mental health course was the best place to begin. I followed this with a few years of clinical experience in psychiatric wards before training to become a qualified psychotherapist.

Before deciding to apply for the mental-health course, I remember reading a magazine that featured medical practitioners who had given up their profession to start an antique shop in Britain. I was astonished at their decision. Most jobs become dull in the end. I plan to become a mental health worker and continue for some years before studying to become a psychotherapist. But this was getting ahead of me.

The short time spent as a temporary unqualified mental health worker made me feel good about helping others in need. I was astonished by my patience and eagerness to listen and learn. I was hoping for a "good enough" mindset and not getting idealistic about my ability to help others.

I have not forgotten my troubling time in England and how much I suffered in the London environment. And at the hands of my romantic notions of life, short perseverance, and not knowing whether I was coming or going.

I understood the problem to be personal, not satisfied for long or easily bored and fluctuating high and low moods. I'd been ready to point the finger at society or myself: wanting too much from life, believing that "eternal happiness" would finally be attainable. All of which might explain the propelling forces of restlessness, which denied me the pleasure of peace of mind.

Now, much older, I've made amends: I cast my dreams to the wind, settled for reasonable goals, received a few modest rewards as nourishment for my inflated ego – and feigned indifference, with the help of music, to the mockery that hails from the ideal ego.

I now wanted to live a simple life with realistic goals. I stopped comparing myself to others; I've become my yardstick, as it were. I hold no grudge against the wrongs I had suffered in the past, at the hands of others, friends, and foes – in England and Guyana.

I was indeed a sensitive soul, though I probably still denied it. I hope I'm not mimicking a hermit, renouncing the pleasures of the flesh. I practise the art of living in "the here and now," an attempt with which to start. I must dispense with the tendency to reminisce–write about all that seems to clear the air.

There were no ifs and buts left or tears to shed, for the well had gone dry, and the sorrow seemed to have worn thin or hibernated. There's a quote by George Eliot that says: *It is never too late to be what you might have been.*

I have reached a point where little things matter, and there remains a tremendous task to help folks live a good life. Ghosts still trouble me from my past, though not as frequently.

I learned a lot about myself from the patients in psychiatric wards and books relating to human problems of the mind, heart, and soul. It's a never-ending process.

Humankind is a paradoxical creature, great thinkers say. It knows and knows not. Life remains too complicated for humankind to master, although many a sage stresses a simple life's rewards.

Epilogue

A layperson's attempt to recount his past was rocky. Harry expected it to be a simple memory chronicle, devoid of emotion and possibly less painful than therapy. Instead, the narrator might have plotted against him: his introspection appeared excessive. However, compared to psychodynamic therapy, it was a walk in the park.

Harry spoke with friends who had received professional therapy and described their experience as an emotional rollercoaster. Some people benefited from the treatment, while others were dissatisfied and blamed the therapist. At the time, he had no desire to endure such an ordeal.

There was no getting around professional therapy once he began training as a psychotherapist. He would have to hope for the best in dealing with his problems. And to learn about his blind spots to better navigate his life through storms and help others professionally so they could help themselves.

Some of his psychologically inclined peers believe that some people are damaged goods. Some people's lives, Harry imagined, remained unchanged, burdened by recurring traumas. The thought of following in his mother's footsteps often brought him comfort.

He thought his unresolved issue was low self-esteem, which caused tantrums. Harry felt remorse after the emotions subsided. The apparition of his father appeared and forced him to accept responsibility.

After he turned forty or older, his situation improved. He learned to understand his father's influence on his life through emotional distance. Harry had to forgive his father to be free. He would later know that it is both the Christian and therapeutic way.

His mother's wish was for Harry to accept himself, his flaws, and all. Recounting this story of lost time had given him some satisfaction. Harry had made peace with the events of his past. "Where the mind goes, the heart will follow," he once read. On the other hand, getting rid of a bad habit has never been easy.

Is it possible to live a simple life in today's world? Harry was afraid of becoming a mimic, but his impersonation of some celebrities may have helped him survive. He seemed content to compromise and accept life as it was in previous years.

BEFORE RETURNING TO Guyana, Harry visited Canada and the United States. His relatives and friends were curious about his life in Sweden. He had shared numerous positive stories with friends and acquaintances. He avoided blaming Sweden because it might have revealed more about him than the country.

He told his family that he had found peace and stability in Sweden and that his life there was reasonable. Harry noted that he had Swedish friends who encouraged him to focus on the positive instead of the negative and that his Christian faith helped him in difficult situations. He told relatives and friends that other people's goodwill quickly brought him joy and that he wasn't surprised by signs of malice.

For Harry, racism existed in Sweden, though it was not as prevalent as in England. He avoids such a discussion because there is rarely a shared understanding. The debate becomes meaningless, with many recriminations and absurdities on the other.

He had Swedish friends and friends of various nationalities, including English. Harry appeared to get along better with the English when he was abroad. He obtained Swedish citizenship and felt connected to the country in some situations but regarded himself as Guyanese, though his feelings fluctuated.

During his two visits to Guyana, Harry couldn't help but feel that he was still a stranger in the country he was born and raised.

To be a global citizen appeared during his two trips to Guyana. Being a global citizen seemed sufficient for Harry Holmes.

Life had moved on.

THE END

I hope you enjoyed this story and would appreciate your feedback - my heartfelt thanks.

Lawrence G. Taylor

Don't miss out!

Visit the website below and you can sign up to receive emails whenever Lawrence G. Taylor publishes a new book. There's no charge and no obligation.

https://books2read.com/r/B-A-WTUD-VBBR

BOOKS 2 READ

Connecting independent readers to independent writers.

Also by Lawrence G. Taylor

The Eternal Struggle: An Amorous Story
Making Sense Of Past Time
Tell Me Who My Enemy Is – a four-act closet drama
Two Girls in a Café
The Ballad of Calle and Maja -- Novella
Getting it Right, if Ever – Romance Novella
Strangers in Another Country
Four Bittersweet Romances & A Four-Act Closet Drama
Dos Chicas en un Café
Darker than Blue -- This Mortal Coil
Religion As Tormentor Of The Soul & Negative Refuge – An Essay
Binky's Reverie
A Day in The Life of Charlie Cheddar
Betty And The Black Puppy
Short Stories Novellas a Closet Drama

About the Author

I was born in Guyana, left there for the UK; worked and studied in London, before taking up residence in Sweden in autumn 1969. In the 70s, I tried my hand at writing fiction, mostly short stories, a four-act closet drama, a novella, and an unfinished novel. I spent two years nurturing the ambition to become an author of some repute. But the going was tough, with no financial security for the future. I shelved the idea of earning a living through writing and got a job as a hospital porter. Later, I got a BA (Eng. & Edu.). After a summer job at a psychiatric hospital, I decided to do a 4-term course for mental-health carers, Following that I completed the first of two stages of psychotherapy education and several short courses in cognitive therapy. After retirement, I did part-time mental health counselling work for several years. In February 2016, my debut book appeared: Strangers In Another Country, a collection of two short stories and two novellas, available in ebook and paperback. On 9th Dec. 2016, I published a novella, The Eternal Struggle: An Amorous Story. In March 2017, Two Girls in a Café, a short story appeared. Making Sense Of Past Time - a Novel available in paperback, and ebook format. Tell Me Who My Enemy Is - a four-act closet drama published this summer (2018). The Ballad of Calle and Maja - a short story published Nov 2018. Getting it Right, if Ever – Romance Novella was published 22nd Aug -19 Four Bittersweet Romances & A Four-Act Closet Drama was published 3rd Nov 2019. In 2020, I published a short story, Darker Than Blue --This Mortal Coil. MY BOOKS ARE UPDATED (Dec 2020). I have a Twitter account @lgt41 and a blog page: lgt41blog.wordpress.com. I'm a hobby photographer, and you can view several of my images at https://www.foap.com/community/profiles/lgt41 I sincerely hope you find my stories enjoyable, and a review of my books would be much appreciated. Lawrence G. Taylor